SAM CRESCENT

EVERNIGHT PUBLISHING ®

www.evernightpublishing.com

Copyright© 2022

Sam Crescent

Editor: Karyn White

Cover Artist: Jay Aheer

ISBN: 978-0-3695-0501-9

SAM CRESCENT

TWICE THE DIRTY

Dirty Fuckers MC, 4

Sam Crescent

Copyright © 2022

Chapter One

Skylar Davies watched her sister as she worked around her kitchen in the diner. Teri Davies, her best friend and sister, was one of the best cooks in the world as far as Skylar was concerned. They both did okay in the kitchen, but then, that was where they had always gone to try to get away from their mother.

"I'm bored," Skylar said.

Teri burst out laughing. "Why don't you go and enjoy the Friday night party? You know you want to. It's fun."

Running fingers through her hair, Skylar glanced out at the busy diner. There were several bikers out there, along with a townful of people wanting their food.

"I think I'll help you."

"You wait tables now?" Teri asked, chuckling. "When did that happen?"

"I can be very reliable, I'll have you know." Skylar winked at her sister, and left to go and join the women who were rushing around. She hated waiting tables. When she was eighteen and in her last year of high school, she had gotten a job like this one, and it had been a nightmare. There was a time that she believed people could be nice. It turned out that people could, providing you didn't have anything wrong with you.

The biggest problem people found with her was her weight. No one liked that she was a size twenty. Her fat ass, big tits, and rounded stomach had always been something for people to use to ridicule her. Not to mention the torture her mother put her through, but Skylar refused to go there.

Her mother was the last person she wanted to think about.

"Everything is okay here, Sky. You're going to be fine," Teri said, coming toward her.

"I can't believe you're running with an MC. I always knew you had a recklessness about you."

Teri threw back her head and laughed. "The Dirty Fuckers MC are my family, babe. They take care of me, and I take care of them. They're more of a family than our own parents. You should give them a shot."

Since arriving in Greater Falls, Skylar had spent every single moment with her older sister. Teri was a beautiful woman, a wonderful person inside and out. Over the years, she had spent a great deal of time trying to protect her, to show her love.

"I don't think I can keep living in the clubhouse though. It's … erm … an experience."

The chuckle from Teri made her smile even more. "Honey, I think it will take a long time for you to get used to. Even now I struggle with it."

"I doubt that."

"Hey, I'm trying to be the big sister here, showing you love and stuff. The guys are amazing, and you will love them. Yes, they fuck around and they fight, but you know what? Deep down, they have a lot of heart."

Skylar looked into the room and saw three of them throwing food at one another.

"Okay, so deep down they are also just children. You've always been good with kids. Show them a bit of motherly love," Teri said, patting her back.

Chloe rushed toward the door. "Teri, we need help out here. I can't keep up."

"It's Friday, and people don't want to cook for themselves. Lazy bastards mean I get money." Teri shoved Skylar forward. "My sister has just offered to help. Isn't she nice?"

Before Skylar knew what was going on, she had a notebook, a pen, and a menu in her hand.

"Just tell them that you're new, and you're finding your way around," Chloe said. "You're an angel."

"I'm not that." Skylar blew out a breath, stared at the diner, and just got straight into it. If they had something bad to say about her size, then, like all the other times before, she would deal with it, simple as that. Approaching the first table, she smiled, and that was how she spent the first thirty minutes, taking orders, and then shouting them out to Teri. Grabbing drinks, and filling up cups of coffee. Dealing with sugar, and other things as well. Chloe kept steering her left, right, and center.

She didn't know what she was doing, but she just kept on regardless, humming to herself as she did.

"Can you deal with the Dirty Fuckers?" Kitty Cat asked.

Skylar glanced over at the bikers, and grimaced. "I don't really know them."

"You're Teri's sister. Believe me, you'll do fine,

and they won't hurt you. Teri has promised to gut them all if they make you cry."

She laughed. "That is my big sister. Always taking care."

"Please, I'm swamped."

Kitty Cat left, and Skylar blew out a breath, and made her way over to the large table. The moment she was there, it all went silent.

Don't panic.

Don't be nervous.

These are Teri's friends.

The ones you've seen completely naked.

"Hi," she said.

"Hey, darling. We see that you're swamped. We'll just have our regular," James said. She recognized him. His wife Cora was sitting beside him.

She nodded, and quickly rushed back to the kitchen.

"James said all of his table would have the regular."

"Okay. That's great. Shit, will you see if Leo and Paul want their steaks medium, rare, or burnt to a crisp?" Teri asked.

"I thought they had a regular."

"They do, but those two like to change their order to suit their own need. Will you find out for me?"

"Yeah, sure." She had never been good at talking to men. Her face tended to flame up, and she looked like a strawberry.

"If you ever want a boyfriend, you're going to have to drop that fat, Skylar. You disgust me."

Walking to the table, she smiled.

"Teri wants to know how you would like your steak?" She looked at Leo and Paul. They were two completely different men, and they were sitting together, chatting. Everyone else was talking, and they hadn't stopped as she approached these two.

"I'm in a medium, juicy mood," Leo said.

She frowned as he looked down her body. Glancing down, she still didn't understand what the problem was. The apron was still clean.

"What's wrong?"

Paul slapped Leo around the back of the head. "Ignore him. We'll take two medium steaks. Thanks, honey."

She nodded and left.

"What is Leo and Paul's deal?" Skylar asked.

"How do they want their steaks?"

"Juicy, and medium. They are weird men."

Teri chuckled. "They are an adorable duo. Believe me, the lucky lady that snags them is in for a right treat."

Skylar paused at the door. "Them?"

"Yep, them. They come as a package deal. You can't have one without the other." Teri sighed. "They are wonderful though. Good men, and I know they're going to treat their woman special."

Glancing back into the room, Skylar saw that the two men in question were staring at her. Offering a smile, she went back to work doing the best that she could to serve and to help her sister out.

Weaving her way through the tables, she couldn't help but remember the horrible names she was called growing up.

Teri was curvy, but it was the kind of curvy that people seemed to gel with. It was an acceptable curviness. Skylar, she was fat, or a cow, or a pig that went oink-oink. So embarrassing passing a table to have that snorted loudly. Yeah, there were many times over the years that she had been so embarrassed by what people had done.

Fortunately, no one said anything or made a comment, and she was able to do her job without fear of some awful noise being directed at her.

She needed to find a job, and working with Teri would be an awesome way to finally get back on her feet.

Greater Falls was a nice place, and she could imagine settling down here.

Before she committed herself though, she would test the waters of being here.

****

"What the fuck did you do that for?" Leo asked, rubbing the back of his head.

Paul rolled his eyes. He hadn't hit the bastard that hard. "Didn't you see how fucking nervous you were making her? She wanted to run."

"I wasn't making her nervous. I was just enjoying the sight before me. She's fucking beautiful." Leo looked toward where she was serving a young family.

Paul knew exactly what Leo saw.

Skylar was a beautiful woman inside and out. Now, they could be wrong. They had been wrong about so many other things before, including Stacey, Cora's friend who had used them for a good time, and moved onto the next man. Last they had heard, Stacey was also screwing someone else now.

They hadn't given Stacey any real thought for some time now. In the beginning, they had cared for her, but that had never been love.

Paul had liked her, and he knew that Leo had as well. They had thought they had found the one, or at least *hoped* they had. That one woman who would be more than happy to have two men in her life.

He and Leo had been together through thick and thin. They had the same taste in women, and there was nothing more arousing than seeing Leo driving inside a woman. Paul could come just from watching his best friend. That was their deal, they came as a package. Two for the price of one. You didn't get one without the other.

Long before they had started looking for a woman to claim as their own, they had both agreed to being with just one. Neither of them wanted to have a woman for themselves. One woman to share, and looking over at Skylar, something inside him just told him that she was the one.

He couldn't pinpoint why he felt that way, but there was something about her. She was different from their other women. Not once had she given them any indication that she even liked them that way.

"You want her, admit it," Leo said, leaning back in his chair.

They often did this, had a conversation between themselves rather than share with the other Dirty Fuckers.

Screwing random women was all fun, but he didn't want to spend the rest of his life just fucking.

He wanted the dream that supposedly most women craved. Yeah, it made him a little fucked up, but he wanted the wife, the house, the kids, the life. He was in an MC, and being a club member would be in his blood for always, but he could have it all.

James had it all.

Drake had it all.

Even the fucking loser bastard Pixie had it all.

He and Leo, they could find something like that. A happiness among them all.

"I never said I didn't."

"Then why hit me?"

"Skylar's not the kind of woman who just jumps into bed with us, Leo. I don't want that. I don't want her for a quick fuck, or to show her how good it can be between us. Look at all of the other women. You wanted Stacey, and we did it your way."

"How do we know Skylar's the one?" Leo asked. "She could be in for a quick fuck. She's Teri's sister. What's to say that she's not just after a good time?"

Paul burst out laughing as Teri slapped Leo up the back of the head as well. She put his plate in front of him, and leaned down to them.

"My sister is nothing like me, and I'm being serious now. If you hurt her, I will cut both of your balls off, and I will make sure that James will let me. Skylar's not some whore you fuck and forget, and don't even think of treating her like that. I will fucking end the both of you."

"Teri, you're crossing the line there," Leo said. "We're club—"

"That is my sister, and you're judging her without knowing a thing about her. Don't for a second think I wouldn't chose her over this club. Don't get me wrong, I'd hate to do that, but Skylar is worth it. You should give her a chance first, before you condemn her to the mountain of sluts you've banged."

With that, Teri walked away.

He always knew that Teri was protective of her sister. Skylar hadn't been in Greater Falls all that long, two weeks maximum. Every time he had seen the lovely Skylar she had been with her sister. Rarely had the two been apart.

There *was* one time he had seen her alone, and that had been at the clubhouse when a couple of the guys hadn't taken the party upstairs. None of them did. They all loved to fuck, and they enjoyed doing it while others watched. Paul and Leo were no different.

Skylar had been standing there, wearing a pair of

the cutest pajamas that had a rabbit on them, and she hadn't walked away, nor had she moved. She had been entranced by the woman in the throes of arousal. Who wouldn't be? When a woman was close to reaching her peak, it was one of the most beautiful sights to behold. One of the reasons he loved sharing women with Leo— besides their unwavering friendship bond—was to see them fall apart in his arms.

He got off on watching, and of course, being part of it all.

Leo sighed, drawing his attention back to him, and not on the sexy, curvy piece walking away from him. "We want her."

"I know we want her. I know what we're going to have to do. Look at her, she thought you were looking at something on her uniform. She didn't realize you were checking her out. Skylar's different. We both know that, and we've got to be careful. I don't want to scare her off, and neither should you," Paul said.

He felt the disappointment coming from Leo in waves. His friend was clearly unhappy with waiting.

It also didn't help that Stacey, Cora's friend, decided to enter the diner at exactly that time.

Cora hadn't been openly friends with Stacey. From what Paul had been told by Ryan, Lucy's son, which was a whole other story, Cora was courteous to Stacey as a colleague. The two had once been friends, but Cora had chosen the club over her friend.

He didn't imagine for a second that was easy to do. In fact, he imagined it was damn hard.

Stacey wasn't alone. Of course she wasn't. It wasn't the gym teacher, it was another guy, someone he hadn't seen before. She stopped by the table, giving them all a smile.

Leo simply glared at her.

Paul didn't feel anything for the woman before him.

Yes, he wanted a family.

Yes, he wanted a future with his best friend and a woman.

Stacey hadn't been it.

In fact, she had been nothing but a couple of holes for them to please themselves. He was a gentleman, and he wasn't about to tell her that. She could think what she liked.

Everyone thought he was devastated at her rejections.

He wasn't. Not anymore. When he looked at Stacey, he was so damn happy that he had dodged that one. She was vindictive, mean, horrible, and it had taken some time for him to see her true colors.

He'd put on an act to help Leo, his friend, who had been devastated.

From the look on his friend's face, he had seen that they dodged a bullet.

"You okay?" Paul asked.

Leo turned to him with a smirk. "Me, I'm all good to be honest. You know, I was just thinking that with her, we dodged a bullet." Leo pressed a finger to his head, and pretended to blow his brains like a gun. "It makes me wonder if I need a bullet to the head for me to understand what could have happened. Could you imagine being forced to be with her? I never saw her spitefulness. She's a bad piece of work."

"I couldn't agree more." Before he could say anything else, Skylar put the rest of the guys' food in front of them. She leaned over the table, giving him a good view of that beautiful cleavage he was dying to get his mouth on.

"Here are your two juicy steaks," she said,

smiling. "Enjoy your meal." She left, and he watched as she handed out the rest of the table's food. Cora got her talking for a few minutes. He noticed that when she was standing, listening intently, she tended to cross her arms beneath her breasts which only served to enhance how damn big they were.

In his mind, he imagined her straddled over him, taking his cock in deep as he rode her hard.

His dick hardened at the thought. Those luscious tits swaying as he drove into her—it was too much of a temptation even for him.

"She's just … stunning," Leo said.

Paul turned to his friend, to see that Leo was in fact looking at Skylar.

Her raven hair was pulled into a ponytail, and her cheeks were slightly red, which he imagined was because of James, not Cora. Skylar was a nervous little thing. What was her story? Teri had always been very hush-hush about her past.

They hadn't even known until recently that she had a sister. It was all a little confusing to him.

In the distance Paul heard Stacey laugh, and she was playing the game she had a few months back. Neither of them were going to fall for it.

"I want her, Paul. I want Skylar."

"Me, too."

Chapter Two

Leo stared across the bar at the Dirty Fuckers MC clubhouse. It was a party, and everything was in full swing. Cora and James were dancing in the middle of the room, along with Drake and Grace. Pixie and Suzy were also dancing. They were the three couples within their club.

As an MC, the Dirty Fuckers were a bit different. They didn't do drugs, nor did they run guns, or try anything else that was illegal. Their one connection to each other was the fact that they had all served under Ned Walker.

Ned Walker was an interesting man. Deadly, vicious, and attached to such a shitload of MCs that it could give someone a headache just thinking about it. Leo had fought his battles, fucked his way through countless women, and relished every single moment of his time as a fighter. From the moment he'd met James and Pixie, Leo knew deep down to his very soul that they were likeminded.

Dirty Fuckers MC was born, and he was a proud member.

They were a club that loved to fuck, that loved to fight, and if anyone got in their way, they would smash them into the ground. Along the way, they'd picked up other people, Teri being one, and Kitty Cat being another, even though she had been close to them a lot longer than anyone else.

Her relationship with Caleb was a bit fucked up. They were a Dom and sub, but slightly more damaged.

Then there was the rest of his club brothers. Leo saw Randy already had a woman between his thighs, sucking his dick. What was interesting about that was the fact Randy had another woman sitting on his face as he licked her pussy.

Daniel, their prospect, was partying it up as well. What that guy didn't know was they had all come to a decision that he had earned the right to call himself a Dirty Fucker. Every time Leo thought about the term "dirty fucker", it always made him smile. He couldn't help it.

Sipping at his beer, he heard the cheer as Teri walked in the door. Right behind her was Skylar. He saw her blush from where he was standing. Even as she smiled and said her goodbyes, he watched as she made her way toward him.

Many of the club guys thought he still had a thing for Stacey. What they didn't know was that he had long gotten over Stacey. Well, it was not even the real Stacey they fell for. The woman they had come to see was selfish, jealous, vindictive, manipulative, and wanted them to compete for her. He and Paul didn't work like that. He had cared for the Stacey he *thought* she was, the illusion she had created, not the woman she actually was, the real her. Knowing the Stacey he thought he cared for didn't exist had made getting over her real fucking easy.

Leo and Paul had been friends for a long time, even back before their time together with Ned Walker. They shared a bond that would never be severed.

"Hey," he said, when Skylar was right in front of him.

Her cheeks were really red, and he saw that she was trying to look everywhere but at him.

"Hey. Did you enjoy your steak?" She frowned, shaking her head. "Forget I said that. I've never been good at making small talk, and it looks like I'm still cursed with that."

"The steak was delicious." He looked past her shoulder at the crowd. "Not your scene?"

"I don't feel comfortable with people having sex. It's … yeah, I'm weird I guess. Some people would love the display that is on. I'll be in my room."

He offered her his beer. "Why don't you come outside and we can talk? You always escape to your room, and you don't need to do that."

"You don't have anyone waiting for you?"

"Nope. Can I tempt you with a candy bar?" he asked, pulling her favorite out of his pocket. He had heard Teri bribing her the other day with one. It was full of peanuts.

She shook her head. "No to the candy bar, yes to the company. I think I need to go to a library or something. I've got nothing else to do right now."

He led the way outside to one of the benches in the far garden of the clubhouse. There were quite a few flowers around, and it was a beautiful sight. He loved it.

"What are you thinking?" he asked.

"This is beautiful." She took a seat, and had a sip of his beer.

"We wanted this place even though it was rundown. This house was connected to the diner, and we think this could have been an old whorehouse," he said.

She burst out laughing. "Really?"

"Well, I like to think it was an old whorehouse. It was a huge home, lots of bedrooms, and we extended it out, and we've got lots of land here as well, which is good. We've got the room to build if we wish to extend further. The garden rocks as well. Pain in the ass to keep on top of though."

"It's a beautiful home. Teri must love it here. She loves anything that allows her to have her freedom. The diner, and then this place, it's like her own personal dream."

"Teri's a good girl." He knew she could be a bad

girl as well. "What's your story then? In case you didn't know, Teri's very secretive."

"There's not much to tell really." She pulled the band out of her hair, letting all the raven locks fall around her face. "We were always close, you know. She's older than me, and she's always been my protective big sister."

He pulled out the candy bar. "Want to share?"

She shook her head. "No. I'm going on a diet."

Leo frowned, looking at her body. "Why?"

"I want to. This is going to be a fresh start, you know. A new me. I've been thinking of looking into staying in Greater Falls long term. I'm hoping Teri won't mind. I've got to talk to her about it. I figured I need a place to stay, so rent money and a job to get the rent money. Teri needed my help tonight, so maybe there's something for me in town?" She shrugged, handing him the beer. She released a sigh. "I think this could be good."

He noticed she avoided talking about anything to do with growing up, which again, he found really curious.

"So, what's your story? Teri told me you and Paul are together? Are you boyfriends?"

Leo burst out laughing. "No, we're not boyfriends."

"But she said that a woman had to settle for the two of you. Doesn't that mean what I think it means?" she asked.

"Nope. It doesn't. Paul and I share women. It's not conventional, but who gives a fuck about convention?"

"What about if one of you falls in love with one, and another falls in love with someone else?"

"That won't happen."

"How do you know?"

"Just do. We're partners, Sky. We may not fuck each other, but we know what we want."

"You've never had a woman independently?" she asked.

He saw she was curious about this. Sipping the beer, he handed it back to her, leaning in close. The scent of coconut met his senses, and he just knew it came from her. He suddenly had an urge to smear chocolate on her skin, and lick. "Yes, we have, but I can tell you in the last fifteen years with Paul, I've not been with a woman without him there."

Her gaze went to his lips, and then back to his eyes.

"Not once," he said. "There's just something about a woman being between us that I can't seem to get out of my mind."

She took a deep breath, and when he chanced a glance down at her chest, he saw that her nipples were erect, pressing against the front of her shirt.

"Then you're going to make a woman very happy. Teri told me that you had your heart broken by that woman I served tonight. Stacey?"

Teri talks a lot.

"I didn't get my heart broken. Plans were changed is all. I'm not pining after her either. She wasn't who we thought she was, and you can't be heartbroken over someone who doesn't even exist." Stacey had turned into just another fuck, but he doubted Skylar needed to hear that.

Suddenly, she pulled away and leaned back, sighing. "I love the sky at night. I really do. I love it when it's clear, and it seems like a never-ending darkness, and I also love it when it's dotted with stars, lighting our paths. It's rather surreal how amazing it all is."

"Amazing what is?" he asked. He was far more interested in watching her.

She chuckled. "Think about it. We're one tiny world in an entire galaxy. I wonder if somewhere out there if there's another world exactly like ours, and right now there's a bunch of people partying, with a couple on the bench, talking about exactly the same thing. It's space, and I find it so fascinating."

"Do these people on this other planet look green with things popping out of their heads?"

She laughed, and he loved that sound. He wanted to keep on hearing it.

"I don't know. But I'm not so narrow minded as to think we're the only species out there."

"Do you believe in aliens, Skylar?"

She winked at him. "Maybe."

Yeah, she was a different kind of woman. One he knew he would never get bored with. Her eyes held laughter, but it held something so much more appealing. She wasn't a woman just after a fuck. He could sense that.

Skylar didn't even realize that he wanted her. Right now, his cock was so hard that moving was causing him pain.

Still, he loved just being with her.

It was refreshing.

****

The following morning, Skylar rolled over and stretched. After her talk with Leo at the bench about aliens and space she had excused herself to bed. Working at the diner was exhausting. Her sister was a damn good cook, so it wasn't hard to imagine a busy diner. Glancing at the clock on the bedside table, she saw it was a little after eight, and she already heard commotion downstairs.

Climbing out of bed, she went to the en suite bathroom, which she loved more than anything else. She didn't have to see anyone just to go to the bathroom to pee. After she'd gone to the toilet, washed her hands, brushed her teeth, she went back to the bedroom.

Pulling her hair up into a bun on top of her head, she put on some slippers, and made her way downstairs. The big pajamas she had on pretty much hung off her body, which she liked. She never liked clothes that molded to her shape. She preferred to hide, to cover everything up so no one could see a thing.

She entered the kitchen, and saw Teri at the table, looking like a monster out of a horror movie. Her eyes looked bruised from the makeup that had run, and she was holding her head.

"You look like death," Skylar said.

"Bite me," Teri said. "I refuse to believe that you're in a good mood. It's not even nine yet, and I'm ready to go back to bed."

"It's all that partying you did last night." She took a seat beside her sister, drawing a leg up onto the chair, and hugging it. "You do know that partying all the time will mean you have premature aging."

Teri rolled her eyes. "Sister, you're supposed to be telling me how gorgeous I look in the morning, not how horrible."

Glancing around the kitchen, Skylar saw that they were the only two up. "You were making some racket this morning."

"It wasn't just me. Suzy and Pixie have just left. Cora left as well. She likes to go out for a run. I don't know why. I think she's a crazy woman. One of those aliens you believed in when we were kids. Maybe that is what she is."

Skylar laughed. "You think anyone who's happy

or perky first thing in the morning is an alien."

"It's part of my charm."

"Shall I get started on breakfast?" Skylar asked.

"Well, yeah. It's about time you did something around here. Everyone thinks I'm the only one that can cook. What they don't know is that you're just as good as me."

Skylar smiled, getting to her feet.

The one thing she and Teri always had in common was their love of food. Growing up with their vicious mother, they had often found themselves at the library, looking through cookery books. They were weird kids, but she wouldn't change the hours spent reading doing anything else.

"There's something I wanted to ask you, actually," Skylar said, pouring her sister a coffee.

"Let me drink coffee. A little warning to you. You start cooking bacon and they will be here. Make sure you make plenty."

Skylar nodded, going to the fridge. "Do you stock everything here?"

"Yes. I also do a lot of the cooking. Most of the time they go to the diner though."

"Are you not opening the diner today?" Skylar asked.

"Later I will. First I need to shift this headache, and I need to remember to stop drinking vodka."

"It's usually not that hard to remember."

"Honey, when you're in the throes of a potentially mind-shattering orgasm, you will do anything."

"You were drinking while having sex?"

"Yep. It's what I do, and I love it. You should give it a try some time."

"I'm not here to start any relationship, or to have

meaningless sex."

She had been burnt in the past by boyfriends, and that was not happening any time soon.

One heartless boyfriend was more than enough for her.

"Shame. So, you and Leo spent some time together last night," Teri said, sipping at the coffee.

"He's a nice guy. Sweet, charming."

"Sexy as hell," Teri said, winking.

She didn't say anything. In a large jug, she started to crack eggs, and then began adding milk, a splash of vanilla as well. Next, she mixed the dry ingredients, and then matched the two. The bowl of pancake mix was huge, and in another bowl, she emptied out a bunch of packets of chocolate chips. Finally, she melted some butter to add into the mix, and that was all done.

"I missed watching you in the kitchen," Teri said.

Skylar nodded at her sister. "It's fun cooking for a large crowd, isn't it?"

"Yep. I do big massive chunks of brisket, spice it up with a delicious rub, and serve it with a spicy sauce. Yum," Teri said. She kissed her fingers and lifted them in the air.

"Now that I can see you're able to think, and if you're able to moan about food, you can listen." Heading to the fridge, she pulled out the bacon, and began to lay the strips on the baking sheets. The only way to cook lots of bacon was in the oven. "I love Greater Falls. I know I've been here a couple of weeks, but I'd like the chance to live here. Do you think you'd be okay with that?"

She hadn't lived with Teri since they were kids. The moment Teri could, she had left their mother, and Skylar had missed her sister so much.

Nibbling her lip, she looked toward Teri, and saw her sister smiling. "You want to live here?"

"Yes. Not in this clubhouse though. I don't think I can handle coming home to what I saw last night. I also don't want to sit around all day. I'd love to have a job, and maybe set my life up here. If you don't want me to do that, then that is fine. I know having one Davies sister is enough."

Teri got out of her seat, and walked toward her. "I couldn't think of anything better. I've wanted you to come here for a long time. I love being here, honey, and I know the Dirty Fuckers will just adore you."

"I can work at the diner if there's an opening as well. I'd like to do something throughout the day, and also at night." Her mother had instilled into her never to be lazy. She hated it.

When she was ill, she hated people fussing around her, and preferred to keep on working through her illness.

To this day, she had never taken a sick day, and that was exactly how she wanted it to be. She wasn't a lazy person.

Never would be.

She loved to work.

If she didn't work, then it always made her feel sick to her stomach.

"She's not here anymore, Skylar," Teri said. "I'm happy for you to relax, and just have some fun."

"And I've done that for two weeks."

"You've been cleaning the clubhouse, not to mention that room. At the diner, you jump right in, and you work. You're not lazy."

"Exactly, so keep me busy. When breakfast is done, I'm going to get dressed and head into town." She glanced down at her bunny pajamas. "I do not want to be walking around like this."

Teri kissed her head, and then sat down. "Ugh, I

feel sick."

"You smell like alcohol." Skylar wrinkled her nose.

The scent of bacon started to fill the air.

"I would start those pancakes if I was you, honey."

The noise of the club filled the air. Within a few minutes, the table started to fill up, and Skylar set to work, creating pancakes.

She was amazed at how much they all ate, a large pan of scrambled eggs, warm syrup, and bacon with the pancakes. She also did some toast. In between feeding the crew, she took a couple of the chocolate chip pancakes.

Feeding a huge crew made her feel warm and fuzzy inside. It was strange, but it was something she could get used to.

Leo winked at her, and she smiled.

He was a nice man, and talking with him had been fun. She could imagine being friends with him for a long time. She hadn't spoken much with Paul, but he seemed just as nice. Oh well, the future at Dirty Fuckers MC sounded quite fun.

Chapter Three

"Where did she go?" Paul asked. He stood in the entrance to the kitchen. Teri had everything fired up, and turned to look at him.

"Into town, why?"

"Why has she gone into town?"

"She's looking for a job." Teri released a squeal, and clapped her hands. "She's going to stay. Finally, after so long I'm going to have my sister with me."

"You do know that sisters are supposed to hate each other, right?" Damon asked, taking a bite out of an apple he had just stolen.

"Screw you, Damon. Not all sisters hate each other. I happen to adore mine, and will do anything for her." She grabbed both of their jackets. "Now get out of my kitchen. It's not sanitary to have you guys back here. Leave."

Paul left the kitchen, and looked around the large kitchen. Leo wasn't around, and he had disappeared while Paul had been in the shower.

Pulling out his cell phone, he dialed Leo's number.

It wasn't that he couldn't function without his friend.

They could do other things without each other.

"Hello," Leo asked.

"Where are you?"

"I am with Skylar. Well, she's inside the library at the moment. We've just been to three different places, and she's given them an application. I think to be honest, she needs to work wherever she feels comfortable. I'm thinking the library though. There is an opening for a part-time person to help deal with customers and stuff."

"How about I join you?"

"You want to spend the day with me and Skylar?"

"I couldn't think of anything better."

"Okay. Get your butt down here, Paul."

He was already making his way out of the diner, ignoring Damon as he spoke. Straddling his bike, he turned the engine over.

"Paul?"

"Yeah."

"I get the feeling that she has been through so much already. I think it would be worth taking our time with her."

Paul paused. "We haven't talked about this."

"We both know we want her, Paul. I'm not going to pretend I don't."

"We'll talk."

"Okay."

Hanging up his cell, he was about to pull out of the diner's parking lot when Damon stopped him.

"Where the fuck are you going? James asked us to help Lucy out today, remember?"

Paul groaned.

With Dane, Lucy's husband—or at least soon to be ex-husband—back, they had been providing some help in buffering the relationship between Dane and his family.

Dane had left his family, just got up one day, and didn't come home for a good few years.

The club had tried to look for him. One of them had even gone out to check out all the leads, but they had come to nothing. The problem with Dane was simple. He would have only ever been found when he wanted to.

Of course, Dane had turned up when Lucy, his wife, had started to move on. She had finally gotten somewhere good with the rancher, Lewis. Even her oldest son Ryan had been dealing with his father's abandonment. Then, in classic Dane style, he had come back out of hiding, and screwed them all over.

Paul released a sigh. "Get Randy to help you. I'll swap, and do an extra next week. I've got to go."

Before Damon could complain at him, he was out onto the main road.

Guilt swamped him, and he stopped his bike and glanced back. Damon had his arms folded, and was waiting.

This was the one part of being in the clubhouse they never passed up.

They had all wanted to vote Dane out, but because he had a family, they had decided to keep him in the club.

The man was an unreliable asshole.

Which is exactly what you're being.

Turning his bike around, he pulled in front of Damon. "Give me a second."

Grabbing his cell phone, he dialed Leo's number. "Hello."

"You're going to have to do this shit without me. I completely forgot that I was on Dane patrol."

Leo laughed. "I already figured that out. I wasn't waiting for you. When it came to Dane we all drew the short straw."

"If the asshole didn't have fucking kids, I'd have buried his ass already. Fine, have fun with Skylar. We've got to talk though."

"We will tonight. Have fun."

"I already know you're going to have way more fun than me."

Pocketing his cell phone, he waited for Damon to straddle his own bike, and then they were heading toward town. Only they veered off, and went down one of the streets toward Lucy's home. It had long stopped being

Dane's when he left.

The moment he pulled up outside of the house, he heard shouting, and he saw Dane's bike.

"Fucking asshole," Damon said.

It was hard for all of the club. Dane had been one of them, but he had screwed that over, and now none of them could trust him.

Climbing off his bike, Paul knocked on the door, and made his way toward the noises. Dane, Lucy, and Lewis were in the kitchen. From the look on Lewis's and Dane's faces, things were not going well.

"Paul," Lucy said, with a sigh of relief. "Erm, Ryan needs some help in the garden. I don't suppose you could help, could you?"

"You don't need me in here?" he asked, looking at Dane. His club brother was an embarrassment to their patch.

Dirty Fuckers MC played hard and partied hard, but they were fucking loyal. That was what they did. They were loyal to the core. Dane had broken that when he left his family.

"I've got this," Damon said.

Nodding, Paul made his way out toward the garden, watching as Ryan was throwing his fists against the punching bag they had installed a few months ago.

"Hey, kid," he said.

Ryan looked toward him, and smiled. "Paul. I didn't know you were coming here."

"Asshole turned up before we could get here. You want to tell me what the fuck is going on?" Paul stood behind the punching bag, and allowed Ryan to have at it.

"Are you sure?" Ryan asked.

"Dude, punch the bag already. Just seeing Dane again makes me want to hurt something. You're his son, and he's betrayed your trust. Tell me you don't want to hit something."

"I do."

"Then be a man. You take that anger, and you channel it elsewhere. Remember, never hurt anyone that didn't hurt you. You never hurt a woman or a kid, or a guy that can't fight back. You have morals." Paul slapped the bag. "Remember all of those points, and it means you have what it takes to be a Dirty Fucker."

Ryan snorted. "Who came up with your name?"

"It was a joint effort." He winked. "Now, get your head out of the gutter. You need to understand and be able to cope with that anger, that rage."

Ryan started to hit the bag. At first it was a light touch, nothing too hard. Paul held the bag, and as Ryan became more confident, and less afraid of hurting him, he really gave the bag some, unleashing all of that anger until he pulled away, sweating, looking exhausted.

"I can't do anymore." Ryan shook his head, and collapsed onto the ground. "I'm a bad person, aren't I?"

Paul sat beside the kid.

"No. What makes you think that?"

"I get so angry sometimes. I want to hit him. I want to hurt him."

"Dane?"

"Yes. It's all him. He's not my father." Ryan shook his head. "I can't let him get close. Not again. He keeps stopping by at the school, and my friends can see him." The disgust on Ryan's face was clear to see. "Then he arrives this morning just as Lewis does, and kisses Mom, and he goes crazy. I don't want to be like him."

Paul sighed. "He's your father no matter what, and I get it. I do. You don't want to be like your father, and you shouldn't have to be. You're a better man than that, Ryan."

"Hitting things, that doesn't make me a good

man."

"No, hitting people who don't deserve it. Now that is what makes you a bad person. You're a kid, and yeah, I know you're a teenager and whatever. Just remember all of us were boys once. Some of us have to deal with that aggression. It's not just you." Paul glanced back at the house. "Is that why they're fighting? Dane couldn't stand to see Lucy with someone else."

"That and Lewis has asked if we would all move in together. Dane's telling them no. He's our father, and he'll have the final say."

"Just because Dane's your father, doesn't mean I don't think he's an asshole." Paul winked, and he heard more shouting. "I have a feeling some ass kicking is going to happen. Do you want to move in with Lewis?"

Ryan glanced around the garden, and then looked toward the house. "I think it would be good. He said he'd teach me how to ranch, and he thinks it would be good for me. I've talked to him about dealing with this."

"Putting you to work is a good way of keeping you out of trouble." Paul ruffled Ryan's hair. "Come on. Let's go and see the damage your dad has caused."

****

"That is a lot of books," Leo said.

Skylar walked out of the library with about ten books, maybe more. A couple were cookery books, and a few more were romance books. She was bored being stuck in all day, and all night. Whenever she had nightmares of the past, they always kept her awake, and she didn't want to spend her evenings thinking about the past. No, she wanted to think of the future, or fluffy romance goodness.

"I intend to do a lot of reading." She had also applied for a position in the library. She was hopeful of the job there. Working in a salon wasn't what she wanted to do with her day. The chemicals always made her nostrils itch, which was weird, she knew that, but it was the way it had always been. "Do you know anywhere else I could apply?"

"Do you know much about the law?"

"Nope."

"Then besides Teri, nope. I think applying in the real estate offices was a big mistake, and the grocery store, let's not forget the law enforcement station, as well. There are just some things you're not going to be able to forget."

She smiled. It had been good to start applying for work. The real estate offices hadn't been about applying for a job though. No, she had asked them for places to rent. The woman there had looked her up and down, and told her no.

There was also the internet to check out as well. She wasn't out of options. At least not yet, and she wasn't going to give up hope of finding somewhere to live.

"So Paul called and he was going to be joining us, but he got held up, so I was wondering what you thought of a little bit of shopping?" he asked. "My treat."

"You want to take me shopping?"

"I want to take you to have some fun. There's a mall near the city. It's a couple of hours. What do you say?" he asked. "We're not on my bike either, so it's all comfort."

"Okay, fine. I'll be happy with that," she said.

He opened up the trunk of the car, and she placed the books in carefully, and then climbed into the passenger side.

Once he was seated in the driver's seat, he started the car and pulled away. Opening the window, she basked in the feel of the fresh air on her face. It was nice to get out into the sunshine.

"Those pancakes this morning were so good," he said.

"I'm pleased you enjoyed them. They're what I make whenever Teri is feeling poorly, and as you saw this morning, she looked like death warmed up."

"She does not handle her liquor well."

"All that partying will catch up to her, but I'm not going to judge. We like to live our lives differently."

"Yeah, have you had anyone in your life then? Someone that we can expect to come back and claim you?" Leo asked.

Skylar laughed. "No, of course not. There's no one waiting for me either. I'm all good and alone." She ran her hands down her thighs. "I mean, I've had boyfriends before, so don't think I've not."

Leo looked over at her.

"What about you? Any girls?" she asked.

"Nope. No one. I am a free agent. Neither has Paul, just so you know. What happened to your last relationship?"

"You're a little nosy."

"I'm curious, not nosy. Besides, friends should know these kinds of things about each other."

"That's what we are? Friends?"

"Don't you want to be my friend?"

He pouted, and she felt guilty. "Of course I do. I'm sorry. I'm just not used to this kind of talk."

"What talk?"

"Friends." It was mortifying actually. She had never had a friend before. Kind of silly really. "I've never had anyone to talk to. Teri has been my best friend."

"She's your sister."

"I don't make friends easily." Understatement of

the decade for her.

"Well, good for you, I happen to be awesome at making friends, and I can guide you into all the awesome things."

"I bet you could." She laughed.

Leo was a fun, loving, amazing guy. He was sweet, charming, and everything that she had hoped to be with one day. Of course that would never happen.

"So tell me about your previous guy. We're friends here, remember. Don't leave out the gory details."

"I met someone. He wasn't … very nice. It ended, and I came here."

"That is so not giving the juicy details. Okay, I'll tell you about mine. So one day, two women walk into a club. They live in town, and two men spot one woman, and she's cute, nice even. One thing leads to another, and the two men share her. She tells them all night how she would love the opportunity to be loved by two men, and how much she could love two men. So these two men decide to give it a shot. At the end of the day, these two men are not getting any younger, and with old age being a factor, they figure it's worth a shot."

Skylar stared at Leo as he told his story.

"Anyway, the next morning, clarity is with you, right? But this woman still tells these two men that she wants forever. Now, both of these men think this woman is exactly who she says she is. She's beautiful, charming, nice, and kind, and she seems to want exactly the same thing that these two men want. A family, a future, love. So, this woman strings the two men along, saying how much she would love to have a family, fall in love, and get everything that these two men one day hope to have. Anyway, you know what sucks for these two men?"

"No. I don't know," she said.

"These two men discover that she was only having a good time, and was using them to get another man. She was cheating on them, and all the time these two men thought they could have hope. Even though the same two men were only doing it for the other one to make him happy. Now these two men have to live with the club thinking they are heartbroken. I guess in a way they were, but more because they were sucked in by a woman's falseness."

"You're not heartbroken?" she asked.

"Nope. I cared about the woman she was *pretending* to be. That woman didn't exist. I was pissed off more than anything. Now that is sharing a past experience, babe. Your turn."

She ran fingers through her hair. Even though she had pulled it up that morning to do breakfast, she had taken it down to go out.

"I had a boyfriend, and at first it was fine. I'm not going to lie, I didn't get chills, or feel much of anything. Being with him was nice, and that niceness changed when I saw his friends. They laughed and mocked him because I was a girl who was fat. I was the fat girl. Yep, that was me. Then he wanted me to lose weight, and he kept constantly telling me exactly how horrible I was. Let's just say that for a long time life has sucked. Anyway, Teri inviting me came at the best or the worst time in my life. There's no one from my past who is going to be coming for me. Don't worry about that." She smiled at him.

Leo pulled into the parking lot of the mall. "I think you're a very beautiful woman, Skylar."

"I'm fat."

He sighed. "You can stop that right now. Some people may think you're fat, but I don't. I think you're a beautiful woman."

She stared at him, and was shocked to see that he truly believed that. There was no humor in his face. Leo meant what he said.

"Thank you." Her cheeks heated. "That is probably the nicest thing anyone ever said to me."

"I noticed you and Teri don't talk about your childhood. I take it your parents weren't exactly loving."

She froze. "I just don't talk about that."

"One day maybe you will trust me enough to talk about it." He climbed out of the car. "Come on, let's go and shop."

Skylar took his hand, and turned him. "Thank you. You didn't have to tell me about your story, but you did. Thank you so much."

Leo smiled, and he leaned in close, pressing a kiss to her cheek. "Like I said to you before. You're going to learn to trust me."

She wanted that, more than anything. Leo was a sweet man, and she hoped one day, she could be able to have someone that she could call a friend.

Chapter Four

Paul was at Skylar's door, and he saw it was partially open. It was a Saturday evening, and Leo was already at the diner waiting for them. His friend had spent so much time with Skylar that he wanted the same chance.

With the door open, he was able to see Skylar. Did she not know that the door wasn't closed? He figured as much because she was walking around in a pair of red lacy panties and a matching bra.

Gritting his teeth, he tried not to give away that he was peeping. She looked so womanly. Her curves called to him, and her tits, they were nice and large. He couldn't wait to have her riding his cock. She would be so perfect for them.

She was just pulling on a dress, and he took a few steps away, then cleared his throat, knocking on the door.

He heard Skylar squeal, and then she was opening the door. "I didn't even know that was open. I'm so sorry if I gave you a show there. Oh, my God, this is so embarrassing."

Her cheeks were beet red, and he didn't like to see her so uncomfortable.

"I don't know what you mean. I was wondering if you'd like some company for the diner. I can be quite magnificent," he said, pushing his hair to one side, and pretending to be a prince.

She laughed. "That's funny."

"I have to say, people don't realize how amazing I am. It's the Dirty Fuckers image I'm afraid."

"Your name is very colorful. I doubt when people see it they instantly think of tough and scary bikers."

"You're right. They probably think of smelly bastards." He shrugged. "It's a name that we all liked, and of course we were all thinking about sex, and how we like it. Dirty, mean, and everything that makes sex good." He leaned against the doorframe, watching her as she pulled on a pair of flats. She stood and smiled at him.

"Good sex. I get it." She smiled. "You didn't see anything then with the door being open?"

He could tell her, and then she would act differently around him. He didn't want that. "I didn't see a thing." Sometimes a little white lie was best. "Leo told me that you had a productive day."

"Yes, we did. It was a lot of fun. At least, I enjoyed it, and I bought some things I probably shouldn't have."

"I'm pleased to hear you had fun."

"I applied for a couple of positions as well. That should be fun."

"Positions?" The only thing going through his mind was having her on her knees, or flat on her back with him riding her pussy hard.

"You know, jobs. I've applied at a couple of places in town. I'm really excited about it. Of course, I didn't find a place to rent, but that's no problem. I'll keep looking."

"You want to move out of the clubhouse?"

"I can't stay here forever, and I don't feel comfortable here all the time. You guys are amazing, and have been very nice to me, and I appreciate it. Just all the partying, and the sex. It takes some time for a girl to get used to."

"You know all the women that are being fucked are there because they want to be, right?"

"I know. I've never been good with the whole personal stuff. There's nothing wrong with it. I'm just a bit weird that way. No biggie." She stepped out of her room, and he offered her his arm.

"Shall we?"

"I'd love to. I am starving. The club seems a bit quiet tonight."

"A lot of us descend onto the diner. Teri is usually swamped."

"Well, I can jump in and help if the need arises. I don't mind doing that." She held onto his arm. "Leo told me what happened between you and Stacey. I'm so sorry."

"Don't worry about it. Neither of us really wanted her. I see that now."

"He said the same thing. That the two of you hadn't been clear on what you wanted, and that had been your downfall. It must suck. I know what it's like to want something, and to be taken advantage of."

He patted her hand. "Don't you worry about me. I'm a big man. I don't hurt easily."

She smiled at him, and it took his breath away. She dazzled him.

Paul wondered if this was what Leo felt when he was with her.

They left the clubhouse and started walking toward the diner. He saw how busy it was, and with the warm weather, the diner had tables outside.

Daniel was there, serving. They had all agreed that he was going to be a patched in member, but that hadn't happened yet. With the drama from Dane, and just life in general, they hadn't been able to find any available time to party.

Also, Daniel's leather jacket wasn't ready yet.

He saw Lucy and her crew of devils were there along with Ryan. Dane was there, as was Lewis.

"Be warned, babe, tonight could hold a little drama. I think you should sit between me and Leo to keep you safe."

"Okay. I don't mind. You're both sweet, and have been so kind to me."

She rested her head against his shoulder, and Paul couldn't believe how much that meant to him.

Get your shit together.

Entering the diner, noise filled the air. Laughter, a child's scream and giggles, chatter, and just a humming of energy.

Leo had saved them two seats, and what fun, they were going to be near the drama. James was there along with Cora, Pixie, and the guys. Joseph was sitting with Drake and Grace. Pixie had his arm across Suzy's chair, her stomach showing her pregnancy.

Paul looked at Skylar, and damn it, she would look so perfect swollen with his kid. Such a tidal wave of arousal rushed through him that it was a relief to finally sit down. He needed to get his head back in the game. First, he and Leo needed to talk.

"Hey, Skylar," Lucy said.

"Hello. Did you have a good day?" Skylar asked.

Lucy glared at Dane, but nodded. "It was fine."

"You're not moving my kids out of that house, and that's final," Dane said.

"Let's not do this here. There are kids, and other people present," Lewis said.

"Shouldn't you be shoveling shit or something?"

Lucy slammed her hand down on the table. "Enough!"

Lewis glared at Dane, and vice versa.

Skylar let out a little breath. "Hey, Leo."

"Hey, princess. How are you?"

"I'm doing great, you know."

"You look stunning," Leo said.

"So anyone going to talk to me?" Paul asked, turning his back on Dane, and smiling at the woman he wanted, and at his best friend.

"I'm so sorry you couldn't join us today," Skylar said. "We didn't really do much. Went shopping, had some lunch, and stuff like that."

"Anyone called you back yet?" Leo asked.

"Nope, no one. I'm hoping for the job at the library. I love being around books. They make me feel happy." She glanced around the room, and Paul watched as she bit her lip. "I'll be right back."

She got up, leaving the seat empty behind her.

"Have you noticed that she always seems to need to work?" Leo asked.

Paul watched her leave, and when he glanced over at his friend, he saw Leo was doing exactly the same. "Yes. I had noticed that."

"It's like she's afraid to relax, and that I don't like."

"Dad, stop," Ryan said, drawing Paul's attention. Ryan was a good kid, but if the club wasn't careful, he would spiral out of control, and it would all be because of his idiot father.

"You think you're cut out to be a rancher's woman. Is that it? You think you can take care of her."

"You know what, I've had enough of this," Lewis said, standing up.

Dane smirked.

"Outside!" Lewis rested his hands on the table, and leaned across, glaring at Dane. "Let's settle this like men. Outside!"

Lewis didn't wait around, and from the look of James, their Prez, he wasn't impressed either.

"Seriously? Couldn't you wait to piss off the locals until after we eat?" James asked. "Let's go outside."

Paul wasn't about to miss the fight, and he and

Leo were the first ones outside.

Lewis was already rolling up his shirtsleeves.

"What do you think? Get his ass kicked?" Leo asked, looking at Lewis.

"Not a chance. He's a rancher. I've seen him in action. Lewis is a tough guy, and I think Dane's fucking stupid if he thinks for a second that he can take him," Paul said. Ranch work was not easy. It was long hours, hard labor, and not for the faint-hearted.

"Are you sure you want to do this?" James asked, going toward Lewis.

"I've had enough of his filthy talk. He has a son present, and yet he's treating Lucy appallingly. He can say whatever he wants about me, I don't give a fuck. To my woman, that I will not stand for." Lewis was focused on the door.

James patted his stomach. "Okay then. Be warned, he's one hell of a fighter."

"I don't wear a leather cut, nor am I a member, but don't for a second think I can't take this."

"He's going to kick Dane's ass," Paul said.

"Pretty much a guarantee. He's not doing it for himself. He's doing it for Lucy."

Paul stood beside Leo as Dane waltzed out. Whatever had happened to their friend? The cocky bastard before them did nothing but disgust him.

There was a time Dane had been like Lewis, and then one day, he'd gotten so sick and tired of responsibility that he'd left it all behind, screwing his way around the world, from what they had been told.

Oh well, Paul for one was looking forward to watching this.

****

"I cannot believe Dane would do this. He's been such a prick since he got back, but this is just stupid."

"He wasn't being very nice to Lucy at the table," Skylar said.

Everyone was standing at the doors and windows to watch the fight. Even Teri had rushed toward the kitchen window and flung it open to watch.

"Why are you watching?" she asked.

Teri shrugged. "This is my club, Sky. Believe me, I want to see what happens so I can help deal with the fallout. Also, this is my fucking diner. I want to see who caused the damage."

Unable to resist, Skylar walked up toward the window beside her sister. Dane, looking really fucking cocky, approached Lewis. "Just looking at him makes me want to see him lose," she said.

"You've got no idea. Lewis is a good guy. He has taken on Dane's kids even when he didn't have to. Ryan needs a good father figure right now more than ever," Teri said.

Skylar winced as Dane threw the first punch. What surprised her was that Lewis didn't go down, and he didn't show signs of it even hurting. That one punch started it all.

Lewis slammed his fist into Dane's gut, and then cut him beneath the chin. Dane elbowed Lewis, then threw a punch to Lewis's face. Lewis moved away, grabbed Dane's arm as it came in for another strike, and twisted it behind his back.

She saw and heard Dane's yell.

"You apologize right now," Lewis said.

"Fuck you!"

Lewis shoved him to the ground.

Skylar expected Lewis to hit Dane when he was down, but he didn't. He stepped back, and waited.

Dane got to his feet, and charged at Lewis, sending him down to the ground.

Teri grunted. "Great, now I cannot see."

"You really do enjoy watching two men fighting."

"It's nothing personal, but, I don't know. Dane deserves it." Teri jumped up, trying to see, and then she didn't need to worry as both Lewis and Dane stood.

What Skylar saw in Dane's hand, which glinted in the light, was in fact a knife.

"Holy shit, the cheating fucker. He's got a knife."

Before Teri could call out a warning, James was there. Dane went to stab Lewis, but James entered the fight and caught Dane's arm, holding it away from Lewis.

Skylar gasped. "Oh, my God. Has he been hurt?"

Teri rushed out of the kitchen and pushed her way toward the center of the circle. Skylar followed her, needing to know that everyone was fine.

James had the knife. "Everyone back inside now. The fun is over."

When no one moved, James yelled the order, and they all started moving. Only a couple of the Dirty Fuckers remained. Leo and Paul moved toward Skylar. They stood behind her, and she loved having them both close. They were two kind men.

"James, what the fuck?" Dane asked.

"Lewis, I cannot apologize enough. Please, go on inside, and take care of Lucy and the kids."

Biting her lip, Skylar watched as James then turned to Dane.

"You are a disgrace to the name of our club." James held up the knife, and shook his head. "How fucking dare you?"

"He's after my woman!"

James shook his head. "You lost her, Dane. You went and screwed your way across the fucking planet, leaving her to fend for herself. The fact you're even allowed near her is a fucking miracle. I suggest you get out of my fucking sight, and you do it now before I end you in this parking lot, and I will, Dane. I will."

Skylar tensed up, and Leo and Paul led her back into the diner.

Taking their seats, she watched as the entire diner was tense.

"You okay?" Paul asked.

"Yeah, I'm fine. Is that what normally happens?" Skylar asked. Teri had told her that she was to sit her ass down, enjoy her meal, and that they would talk about her working. Until then, Teri wouldn't hire her, if she couldn't even follow simple instructions. Her sister was a hard ass at times.

"No, it's not always like that. Dane's special," Leo said.

"There's a history there that is going to take more than one dinner to understand. Let's not talk about him anymore," Paul said. He took a sip of his water. "So, you're hoping to stay in Greater Falls."

"I am. I'm really looking forward to it. Do you like it here?" she asked, curious about the two men. She found herself looking between them. Leo and Paul both leaned on the table, smiling at her, and she leaned back in her chair so she was able to look at them.

"We do now," Leo said. "At first, we didn't know if we'd be able to stick it out, did we?"

"Nope. We've not been known for sticking to one place for a long time."

"What about Ned Walker?" Leo said. "He has to be the longest we've stayed in the same place."

"What's Ned Walker?" Skylar asked.

"Only the biggest, deadliest motherfucker around," Paul said. "He commands the underground fighting ring in Las Vegas. No one knows him, and yet everyone who is anyone does. He's got a reputation, but he's a fair man. He's also old as fucking sin."

Leo pressed a finger to his mouth. "Sh, he doesn't like anyone speaking shit about him."

She giggled. "He sounds … interesting."

"He's a ladies' man, or at least he was the last time we saw him a few years back. He's connected to another MC through marriage though, and you do not want to mess with them," Paul said. "They're a good bunch though. They just seem to attract drama like a soap opera, and that is not our scene."

"Who is this other group?" she asked, intrigued, but she just wanted to keep them talking.

"The Skulls. They are badass, and believe me, they know how to set fires under pretty much everything," Leo said.

"I've never heard of them." She shrugged. "You're the only MC that I've known of."

"Yeah, well, hopefully we can tempt you to stick to just us." Paul winked at her and placed a hand on her knee.

Pleasure rushed through her at that single touch. She looked at his hand, and bit her lip.

It's not like that.

Pushing any thoughts of something more intimate to the back of her mind, she looked at the two men. They could be friends. That was clearly what they wanted.

Someone clearing their throat had Paul pulling his hand away. Looking up, Skylar saw the other woman that they had both spoken of, Stacey.

"Well, well, well, you're the flavor of the month right now. I should have known really. It's fun while it lasts, but believe me, honey, you don't want to be the laughingstock of the town with you just moving here and all," Stacey said, hand on her hip.

The sound of a chair pushing out had Skylar watching as Cora approached. "You've got no right talking to the club like that. Get gone, Stacey."

Skylar was further embarrassed as Teri came out, wiping her hands on the cloth.

"Run along, Stacey," Paul said. "You're here to cause trouble, and we're not in the mood."

"They are still not over me. If you think for a second that they are, you're wrong. They both want me, and they are so upset that I didn't want them."

Cora grabbed Stacey's arm, and gave it a tug. "Don't for a second think you can test me."

"I thought I was your friend," said Stacey.

"Friends don't try to get other friends fired, and they also don't try to tear apart their marriage." Cora shoved her away. "You're no friend of mine."

"Get out," Teri said, raising her voice.

This was just getting even more mortifying as the minutes passed.

"Excuse me?"

"You heard me. I got rid of your ass before, and then you decided to come on back—well now I've changed my mind. I don't want your skank ass, or your custom. Anyone else got a problem with me throwing the trash out, you can leave right along with her," Teri said. "This is my diner. They are my family, and that is my sister. Try me, bitch, and let's see how far you can really be pushed." Teri stepped right up to Stacey.

Skylar had seen her sister fight before, and no one had ever bested her. Personally, she hated violence, and would do everything she could to avoid it.

Stacey stepped down, and walked away.

Wow, two dramas in one night. Smiling at Paul and Leo, she saw they looked worried, and she didn't understand why.

Chapter Five

Dane couldn't believe what he had fucking done. Never in all of his life had he played dirty like that. The moment Lewis had called him outside, he had been ready to fucking kill the bastard. If he was being honest with himself, he had truly believed that it would be an easy fight as well.

Lewis was a damn rancher. There was no way he'd be able to win, but his punches were fucking hard, and Dane had been losing. In the back of his mind he had thought for a second that he could win back his wife.

You lost that when you fucked the first woman that wasn't her.

Lighting up a cigarette, he stared up at the sky. He had completely fucked up, and it was all his fault.

His kids, his wife, the club he loved more than anything were different, and it was all his fault.

"Dane," Lucy said.

He turned to find her standing with her hands locked together in front of her. Her hair was pulled up into a ponytail, and the black dress she wore molded to every curve of her body. He had spent so many hours kissing her body, loving every inch of her. There was a time he'd have had her laughing, and crying out his name right before he took possession of her, claiming her all for himself.

She folded her arms, and he saw the disappointment in her eyes, and that hurt more than anything.

"I'm sorry," he said. "I shouldn't have done that."

"You pulled a knife. Not only that, but your disrespect. How could you do that?"

"I wasn't thinking."

"For crying out loud, Dane. Our kids were there.

Ryan was there."

"He fucking hates me."

"And whose fault is that? Mine? I'm not the one that walked away. I'm not the one that decided being a damn grownup was too much for him."

"You didn't exactly wait around for me."

"Oh, you fucking asshole." Before he knew what had happened, she had reached down and grabbed a stone, launching it at him. "How dare you? I waited years for you, Dane. I stayed up late at night, and got up early in the morning, hoping that you would walk through the damn door. I was scared that you had died. We have kids, Dane. Responsibilities. Bills, debts, you name it, we had it, and you walked away. Ryan, he would come home and look through every single room. He even went to the cops for them to put a search out for you. You didn't wait for me. You *left* me." Tears were shining in her eyes, and he had been the monster to put them there.

"Lucy?"

"No. You don't get to judge me. You cheated, Dane. Not me. I've done everything I can to keep this family together, and you go and try to destroy the one bit of happiness? Why?"

"Because you're mine."

"I stopped being yours the moment you touched another woman. Now I'm going to give you a choice right now. I've never given you one of these. You either get your head out of your ass and move on, because I am. Or leave and don't come back."

"My kids?"

"You left them before. I don't want them to be without a father. They deserve someone who isn't going to hurt them, Dane. If all you're going to do is hurt them, then leave. I didn't think I could survive without you, but I did. I moved on. You're still our children's father, and I could never take that away from them."

"Even though you're giving me an ultimatum?"

"For the sake of them, Dane. That's what I'm doing. Open your damn brain. You would have killed Lewis tonight with all those people watching. They're my kids, and I want what is best for them. Decide."

He watched as she turned her back on him and started to walk away.

"I love you, Lucy. I will always love you. I can't just leave."

Lucy turned toward him, and sighed. "I don't. You're the father of my kids, and I guess there is a part of me that will always love what we had. But I don't love you anymore, Dane. I can live without you. I have. I'm in love with Lewis."

With that, she left.

Stumbling back, Dane sat down on the ground.

He didn't know how much time passed before James was in front of him.

"Make that choice now," James said.

"You heard everything."

"You think I'd let Lucy come here alone when you pulled a knife on a man you were disrespecting?" James grabbed him and hauled him up. "You make that choice right now. You get on your bike, give me your fucking cut, and you leave. You do not come back, and you stop being a Dirty Fucker. You cease to exist to this club."

The very thought made Dane sick to his stomach. Even when he left, he was still a Dirty Fucker.

"Or you stay, and you learn to live with the fact you lost everything for being a selfish bastard. But I swear to you, Dane. You have a repeat of what happened tonight, and I've got a special patch just for your sorry ass."

"You'd kill me? You're not like that, James."

"You don't know me, Dane. I know what I need to do to get jobs done. You won't be the first fucker I've buried in a grave, and I doubt you'd be the last. Test me and see."

He didn't want to test his Prez.

There was Ryan.

His babies.

He'd been out of their lives for so long that they struggled to be near him.

The one thing he wanted back was his kids.

"I want to stay."

"Then pick your game up." James held the knife up to the light. "I'll be keeping this, Dane. Don't for a second think I'm afraid to use it."

****

"That was more drama than I could stand tonight," Leo said, clinking his beer with Paul's.

"Stacey's a problem. She thinks we've got a thing for her. I've got to ask, do you?" Paul asked.

Leo shook his head. "I've not had a thing for her ever since she tried to fool us. I'm pleased she showed her true colors before our feelings for her grew. No, I don't have a thing for her, and I've not for a while. We both want the same thing, don't we? A family."

Paul nodded. "Yes, I want a family, and for a second I did think it could be possible. Then she behaved the way she did. I was fooled, and I think that is what bugged me the most. I didn't see it until the last minute, but that's my problem."

Leo couldn't agree more. "So we're on the same page. Neither of us want Stacey, nor do we love her."

"Nope. She's a first-class bitch." Paul took a long sip of his drink. "I love a good cat fight and all, but I wanted to see Teri and Cora go all super power on her."

Leo burst out laughing. He couldn't blame Paul. "The way she had looked at Skylar, if she had been a guy I'd have fucked her up."

"Yeah, me too," Paul said. "So I guess we should talk about our feelings for a certain sister."

"Teri scares the shit out of me."

Paul laughed. "I don't mean her. I mean her sister."

"I know who you mean." Leo sat beside his friend and stared up at the clubhouse. The light in Skylar's room was on, and he wondered what she was doing. Probably reading one of those romances she had gotten from the library. "I want her, Paul. I enjoy being with her. She's so sweet and charming."

"She smells like coconut, and I just want to pour chocolate sauce over her, and lick her body."

"You two are horny bastards, you know that right?" Teri said, moving away from a darkened corner. She was sucking on a lollipop and smiling. "So you two douchebags have finally seen that my sister is worth your time."

There was something in her smile. Leo didn't know exactly what it was.

"You invited her here," Paul said.

"Correct," Teri said. "And I wonder why I did that."

"Are you playing matchmaker?" Leo asked.

"I know my sister is a damn good woman. She's been hurt a lot in the past, and I've not liked any of the men who she's been with. They haven't deserved her. I'm hoping you two could be different."

Leo took a sip of his beer as Teri approached. "I want to help you. Do you like Skylar?"

"Yes, we do," Paul said, answering first.

"I do. She's ... beautiful."

"Exactly. Now Skylar is a hard nut to crack, if you get my meaning. She sees you as friends. It's going to take some convincing to prove to her that you want something else."

"We can do it," Leo said. He stood up from the table. "I want to be with her. I want to give her all the kinds of love that she deserves, that she needs." Their shopping trip had shown him a lot. She had bought some dresses, and he noticed how she covered up the size tag, and how she always changed the topic when it came to growing up.

"If you're going to help us, you need to give us something," Paul said. "What's with her deal always working? I don't get it."

Teri sighed. "I'm not going to tell you everything. That's not my story to tell, and I wouldn't do that to my sister. Let's just say that if she wasn't doing something … productive, she would get punished. Skylar struggles to be sick. She can't stay still for all that long. She also doesn't watch movies either. She can't. You will also know that her legs bounce in the car if she's forced to stay still for too long."

"There's more to it than that," Leo said.

"I didn't say there wasn't. Let's just say that when she needed me most I wasn't there. I want to give her a life that I couldn't when we were younger. That is my fault, not hers. I want her to be happy. I will help you when I can. I won't tell you her story. I can't." Teri turned and left, leaving him with more questions than he had before.

"She's full of wonders, isn't she?" Paul asked. "At least we know that Skylar's got demons in her past."

"I've got a feeling she's still living with them." Leo had an idea what it was. "I think it has to do with her weight. I don't know why, but she's … I don't know.

Something about her when we went shopping. She wouldn't let me carry the clothes that she bought or help her in anyway. It was strange."

"I figured her weight was a problem. I love her curves, and those tits, I can't wait to get my hands on her. Damn, can you imagine those juicy thighs wrapped around you?" Paul moaned. "I can't wait to sink inside her and hold her close."

Leo's own cock started to thicken at the thought. "Together we do this."

"Good. I already called ahead by the way," Paul said.

"To what?"

"To the real estate place. Skylar didn't go in asking for a job. She wanted a place to rent. I told the woman to refuse her and I paid her off. We don't want Skylar leaving. Can you imagine trying to keep up with her? She's always moving around. It's next to impossible to keep an eye on her now."

Leo groaned, rubbing his eyes. "Why didn't you tell me about that?"

"I didn't think it would matter."

"You're a pain in the ass, Paul. Now we've got a secret, and I'm guessing she has trust issues already. Ugh! I could fucking throttle you." Leo got to his feet, and walked away.

"I did what I had to do."

"You're officially the biggest pain in my ass." Leo walked away. It wouldn't be a big deal, but he didn't know how Skylar would view it. She wouldn't be so willing to open up to them. He only hoped they got her to fall in love with them before they told her the truth. *Stupid Paul.*

****

Paul knew he had fucked up the moment he told

Leo the truth. He didn't want to keep anything from his friend, and he had never been good at keeping secrets. *Crap.* He shouldn't have told that woman to turn Skylar down, but what choice did he have? Rubbing his eyes, he made his way out of his bathroom. His bed was calling him, and he was so tired.

Dropping down onto the bed, he closed his eyes, and darkness fell.

He woke up to the sound of a scream, and then a whimper. Lifting his head off the pillow he saw it was a little after four. Clearing the sleep from his eyes, he lifted up, and listened. Another whimper, and a cry.

Getting out of bed, he left his room and moved toward Skylar's. The noise was coming from her.

Leo came out of his room, and frowned at him.

"She's having a bad dream."

"Please, Mommy. I'm hungry. Please, I hurt. Make it stop."

That was it. He had heard enough. Hearing Skylar in pain or at the very least hurting was more than he could take. Opening the door, he charged inside, and found Skylar tossing and turning.

"Wait," Leo said.

"I'm not letting her go through whatever hell she's going through." He touched her shoulders. "Baby, wake up. You're fine. You're in Greater Falls. You're safe."

She tossed, and then gasped awake. He cupped her face, stroking her hair, trying to offer her comfort.

"Paul?"

"That's right. You're at the Dirty Fuckers MC clubhouse. You're safe. You're fine."

She took several deep breaths, and nodded. "I'm fine. I'm fine."

"That's right. You're safe."

Leo closed the door, drawing their attention toward him. "You were having a bad dream, honey."

Skylar shoved her hair off her face and rubbed her eyes. "I'm so sorry for waking you. It must have been the fighting tonight. I haven't had bad dreams for some time."

"You were crying for your mother," Paul said.

Her face seemed to go a little pale.

"Yeah, well, I don't know why. Again, I'm really sorry for screaming and waking you up."

"I don't mind. I didn't have anything else to do," Leo said. "Sleep can wait until we're dead, right?"

Skylar laughed. "I shouldn't laugh. That is an awful thing to say."

"But it's the truth, right? We're all going to be dead, and then we can all party."

Paul stared at his friend. "There are times you really need to be silent."

Leo shrugged. "I'm only saying what you're all thinking."

"No, I can promise you that is *not* what I'm thinking. I'm tired, and I need to sleep now," she said. "Thank you so much for coming and checking on me." She took his hand. "Thank you, Paul, for waking me up."

He felt the fine tremors in her hand, and he held her tightly. "You have nothing at all to be afraid of. Me and Leo, we've got your back, baby."

"You're so sweet to me." She lifted his hand, and pressed a kiss to his knuckles. "Thank you."

The action was tender, gentle. He reached out and stroked her cheek.

"I've got a suggestion," Leo said, coming to sit on the bed.

"What?" Skylar asked.

"You've had some bad dreams, and we've all

seen the drama tonight. This bed is big enough. What do you say to Paul and me sleeping with you tonight? One on either side, and then we can be here to help with any of your dreams."

Paul glared at Leo. Yes, he wanted to sleep with Skylar close, but the last thing he wanted was to scare her.

"You wouldn't mind?"

"Nope. We wouldn't mind," Leo said. "Right, Paul?"

"I don't mind. I think it would be good. You look a little shaken, and I don't like the thought of you being alone, and maybe a little afraid. Leo and I won't overstay our welcome. If you want us to leave we will."

"That is so sweet. Thank you." She eased down the bed and lifted the blanket. "I've never had two men in my bed. I've not had anyone offer to sleep with me to help ward off any more nightmares. You two are the sweetest."

As Paul climbed into the bed, the last thing he was feeling was sweet. In fact, he was feeling guilty because he had done something that wasn't sweet, not at all. Damn, no wonder Leo was pissed at him. Rolling over, he saw that Skylar was turned toward him, and smiled at him. "Thank you." Then she rolled over, and thanked Leo.

She settled on her back, and Paul couldn't stop looking at her.

This was a weird kind of torture.

The woman that had been appearing in his fantasies was now lying beside him. His best friend was beside her, and neither of them could touch, at least not yet. Time passed, and he knew she was sound asleep by how relaxed she had become. Her body had just gone completely soft.

"She's beautiful. I can't get over just how much she is." Leo stroked some of her hair away from her face. "She's the one."

Paul saw it as well. "She's had a hard life."

"Yes. She's not used to being treated like a queen. I think it's time we change that, don't you?"

"Yes. I do." Paul rested his head on the pillow, knowing he would gladly spend the rest of his life treating her exactly like she deserved.

Chapter Six

Skylar opened her eyes, and became aware of not one but two arms crossed over her body. Frowning, she turned her head and saw Leo on one side of her, and then Paul. She tried to remember what happened the night before, and slowly, it started to come back to her, little by little.

They had heard her bad dream, and came to her room to comfort her. She hadn't wanted to go back to sleep straight away. The memory of her mother was so clear to her even after all this time that it scared her. She didn't like to be controlled by her fear, and yet that was exactly what she was being.

Licking her dry lips, she held onto the bedding, lifting it up to cover her mouth. Morning breath was so horrible, and there were two men in her bedroom.

She was wearing pajamas like she did every single morning.

"What on earth are you doing?" Leo asked, making her turn toward him.

"You're awake."

"You tugged on the blanket. I didn't exactly have much choice in being awake." He winked at her. "Did you sleep well?"

"Yes, I did. Thank you." Her cheeks were heating.

"Why are you getting embarrassed?"

"Well, I had not just you, but Paul here, kind of like a security blanket."

He chuckled. "I was hoping as a big fluffy teddy bear."

She smiled along with him, but kept the blanket over her mouth.

Leo reached out, tugging the blanket down.

"Don't worry so much."

"I can't help it," she said, and then covered her mouth.

Leo coughed, grabbed his face, and pretended to collapse to the bed dead, doing some weird twitching thing.

She couldn't stop laughing at him.

"He's a goofball in the morning, and I'm trying to sleep here," Paul said, suddenly lifting up, and dropping onto her chest, making her ooph out some air. He wrapped his arms around her waist, and his head was resting against her breasts.

"And he hogs the bed. Look at him, he has no respect for personal space at all," Leo said, and he was suddenly there, smiling at her. "Watch this."

She saw the glass of water at the last minute. She gave a scream and then the water was over the two of them, and she covered her face.

Paul sat up with a roar, grabbed a pillow and started to hit Leo repeatedly with it. Working her way down the bed, she fell out of the bottom, and then began to hit Leo with the pillow she had taken with her.

He caught her around the waist, lifted her up, and placed her on the bed. She screamed, and then laughed as he began to tickle her.

"Stop, stop!" She yelled for him to stop as the laughter was just too much.

Next, Paul joined in.

Laughter consumed her, and after several minutes passed, they both collapsed to the bed.

"Now that was a fun way to wake up," Leo said.

"You have completely soaked my bed," Skylar said. "How am I going to sleep here tonight?"

"That's easy. My bed is just as big as this one, if not bigger. I say we all party in my room tonight."

Skylar turned to Leo. "You want to have a sleepover?"

"Have you ever been to one before?"

She shook her head. "No, I never have. I was never invited over."

"Then you are in for a right treat because I can say that I throw the best sleepovers. What do you say, Paul? My bedroom, sleepover. I'll go and rent some movies. Actually, no movies, and I think we could play some games."

"I like playing games. I've never been good at watching movies. I would love to have a sleepover," she said, smiling. It was a Sunday, and she'd intended to spend the day with Teri. "I'm going with Teri to the diner this morning. I better get ready."

"No worries," Paul said, leaning back against the bed. "I don't mind the show. Get changed in that red shirt I've seen you wear."

His gaze traveled down her body. Leo slapped him. "Let's go and give the lady some space."

She laughed, watching them both leave her room reluctantly.

For the first time in her life, she had woken up with a smile, actually looking forward to nighttime again.

She had never been to a sleepover, and she was curious what Leo had planned. It could be fun, or a nightmare. Either way, she needed to air her mattress now that it was soaked through. Even if it was dry, she wanted to experience one sleepover, even if it is in adulthood.

Thirty minutes later, she met Teri at the door, and they both left the clubhouse, making their way toward the diner.

"You're very chipper today," Teri said.

"I know this is going to sound crazy, but I have a

feeling I could become very good friends with Leo and Paul."

"That's not crazy sounding at all. I know for a fact that they are both amazing. So what has brought on this change of heart, if you don't mind me asking?" Teri asked.

"I had a nightmare last night, and they were both so sweet, they stayed with me."

"Nightmares?" Teri paused. "This is the first one, right?"

"Yeah. I think it was caused by the fighting last night, and that thing with Stacey. Do you think she loves them?"

Teri shook her head. "No. She just wants to rub it in their faces that she's moving on, but if you ask me, I think she's pissed that they don't seem to care. I never liked her anyway. She's a fucking bitch."

"You think most people are fucking bitches," Skylar said.

"Don't worry about Stacey. Women like her—she will get what is coming to her. She lost Cora as a friend." Teri shrugged.

They made their way into the diner, and Chloe had just pulled up. "Hey," she said, smiling at them.

Skylar liked Chloe. The other woman was so sweet and kind. She was also dating some lawyer.

"Hey, honey. How's Fluffy?"

"Fine. He's a little monster. He chewed up Kitty's brand new shoes."

"Oh, no."

"Yeah, they were a gift from Caleb, and she's worried that he'll think she did it on purpose because of the crap that is going on between them. He chewed Richard's jacket as well." Chloe wrinkled her nose. "I got a replacement, but I don't know if he'd know."

"This is why I don't get connected with men if you know what I mean," Teri said.

Skylar knew her sister enjoyed a varied sex life, and she had never judged. Her sister always did what made her happy, and relationships never had.

"I'm going to head to the toilet. I got to pee," Chloe said.

Teri entered the kitchen and began firing up the ovens.

"You don't wonder what it would be like to love just one of them? To have one look at you as if you were their entire world?" Skylar asked.

Teri sighed, and turned to her sister. "I love you, Skylar. Me and love, it's not meant to be." She kissed Skylar's head. "So, I'm thinking part time. When do you think you'll hear from the library?"

"I'm hoping tomorrow. You don't mind me sticking around and, you know, invading your space and all?"

"Skylar, shut up. If I minded I wouldn't have invited you out here. Remember that, babe." Teri put on her apron. "How about you make those chocolate pudding pots that I love so much?"

"They're on the menu?"

"Nope, but I want to do a taste test to see how they go with the customers. I love them, but some people have weird taste and it drives me crazy." Teri shrugged. "Taste buds is one of those things that will drive me crazy. 'Ew, this has garlic in, yuck, chili, I don't like runny egg, I don't like cilantro. It's too spicy, it's not spicy enough.'"

She listened as her sister complained, laughing. "You're the one that wanted to be a cook."

"Yeah, well, I love everything, and no one else does. I'm cursed that way."

"I will get started on the pudding pots, miserable." She slapped Teri's ass on the way past toward the fridge. Grabbing cream, milk, and eggs, she headed back to the kitchen, where Teri already had a gloved hand into some meat mixture.

She had missed this so much.

The best part about being with her sister right now was she knew her mother wasn't about to come home to ruin it.

****

Leo checked his bedroom one final time, happy with the way he had changed everything, creating a tent.

"What are you doing?"

"You heard her. She's never been to a sleepover. You tell me what is the first thing you think of at a kids' sleepover."

"Popcorn."

"No, there's always a tent, or something like it, and ta-da." Leo opened up the door. "This is awesome, right?"

"What if she means an adult sleepover?" Paul asked.

"Ugh, you're no fun today."

Paul held his hands up. "Did you know that James gave Dane an ultimatum?"

"He drew a knife. I wouldn't expect anything less. He's driving me crazy. I'd vote his ass out the first chance I get," Leo said. He grabbed the board games, and placed them on the floor. Next, he opened a bag of premade popcorn, and placed snacks around the bed.

"I don't know if this is gross or not," Paul said.

"I'm setting the scene. We've got to be careful tonight. I want us to be friends, but I want to have the whole friends with extras." He held up a teddy bear he had found in her room.

"Seriously?" Paul asked.

"You know, I'm trying here. What are you doing for this?"

"I ordered pizza."

"Wow. Her sister is one of the best cooks around, and you order pizza. You really don't think some days."

"What's going on with you two?" Damon asked, coming inside the room. "Neat, you created a little fort. Didn't you two realize that you're like, old now?"

"Told ya," Paul said.

"Damon, if a woman you really want to be with told you that she had never been to a sleepover before, and you want to make her wishes come true, what would you do?" Leo asked.

Damon tilted his head to the side, pursed his lips, and nodded. "Yep, I'd do what Leo was doing, Paul. Sorry, man, it's a neat fort. This for Skylar?"

"Yep. She's never had a sleepover before, and I wanted to, you know, make it special, and memorable."

"I know she's working hard at the diner tonight. She may not be such good company."

"Leo tipped water over her mattress. Staring at this, it makes me wonder if you planned it," Paul said, brow raised.

Holding his hands out trying to look innocent, he smiled at his friend. "I'm just trying to help."

"You little sneak," Damon said. "Good luck, boys. I hope you get the girl."

Once they were alone, Leo stepped back and was more than pleased with his job. "I did good."

"Did you go to many sleepovers growing up?" Paul asked.

"Nope. You?"

"Nope. I have a feeling her issues are with her mother." Paul pulled out a picture. "I found this in Teri's bedroom drawer."

Leo rolled his eyes. "You're sneaking around now."

"I was doing laundry, and this was poking out of a drawer."

Leo took the picture from his friend, and looked at it. There was no mistaking Teri, nor Skylar.

Standing behind Skylar was a hideous-looking woman, and even as he looked at the picture, he saw the woman held onto Skylar rather tightly.

"That's her mother," Paul said, taking the picture, and flipping it over.

On the back, it named "mother, father, Skylar, and me".

"She called out for her mother last night," Leo said. "Teri told us she had nothing to do with her parents. Do you think Skylar's in touch with them?"

"No. Last night she pleaded for her mother to *stop*, Leo. She didn't beg her mom for help. It wasn't that kind of cry."

Leo sighed, feeling an overwhelming sadness consume him. "You've got to stop looking at shit like this. Skylar will tell us in her own time. Between this and the apartment renting, you could cost us this woman. I don't want to lose her."

Paul took the picture. "I think this is going to be amazing."

"That is the hope. If only you would stop being so nosy."

Paul held his hands up. "I can't help it. I want to know everything, and I've never had the best patience."

"Don't I know it? Now, stop snooping."

He watched his friend walk away, and Leo frowned. If Skylar was hurt by her mother, would she ever talk about it? Teri wouldn't, and he had seen the guilt inside her eyes when she spoke.

Running fingers through his hair, he decided to put it to the back of his mind. Time to go and collect his woman.

Closing the door, he made his way toward the diner, and Skylar was just leaving as he arrived.

The moment she saw him, she smiled. "Hello," she said.

"Hey, baby. Good day at work?"

"Yes. My sister is going to let me work part time there, so yay."

"Don't worry about somewhere to live. Me and Paul never have. The clubhouse isn't so bad."

"That's because you have sex on hand. There are so many women who want that fantasy of having any man they could."

"You don't have that same fantasy?"

Her cheeks were a nice shade of pink. "I never said that."

"Ah, so you can be tempted to join us in sin?" he asked, taking her arm, and linking it through his.

She wrinkled her nose. "Sex is one of those things that I've never seen the point of. It's gross, and for the most part, it wasn't exactly satisfying."

Leo turned to her. "Then you've been doing it wrong."

She laughed. "It's not exactly hard to do. One things goes into the other, and boom, done."

He rolled his eyes, and taking her hand, he moved her to a secluded part of the diner. Pressing her against the brick wall, he stared into her eyes. They were open in shock.

"What you have just described is something similar to baking a cake. Wet ingredients into dry."

"Isn't that what happens?"

He chuckled. "Oh, baby. Believe me when I say to you that there will never be a part of you that is dry when I get my hands on you. You'd be completely soaking wet. You see, for me it's not about putting my dick into a pussy. It's about making my woman moan, whimper, and beg for more. I don't just want a quick fuck. I'd want to possess her so that every single move she took, she would know who owned her."

He watched as her eyes dilated. She was intrigued. Glancing at her tits, he saw her nipples were poking against the fabric of her shirt.

"There would be no way that you would come away thinking that sex was anything but amazing." He leaned in close, wanting more than anything to take the kiss that he imagined she would freely give. "Maybe you should explore your options."

Even though it was the last thing he wanted to do, he pulled away.

She released a breath.

"I have a surprise waiting for you back in my room."

Skylar nodded, taking his hand. He had unnerved her. It was good, but now he needed to keep her on her toes, which he wouldn't do if Paul kept snooping. They needed to work together on this.

Entering the clubhouse, he found Paul already there.

"Hello, princess," Paul said, taking her hand, and pressing a kiss to her knuckles.

"Paul," she said, saying the name with a sigh.

"Leo has gone a little overboard. If you don't like it, it's entirely his fault. If you do, I helped."

She laughed. "You are so funny."

"Come on," Leo said. "Let's see which one he'll claim."

Taking the steps, he made his way toward his room, and opened the door. Paul quickly covered her eyes, and slowly they entered the room.

Closing the door behind her, Paul lowered his hands, and Leo heard her gasp.

"Oh wow, this is amazing."

"Totally my idea," Paul said.

Skylar shook her head. "You already gave away that this was totally *not* your idea. This is awesome." She knelt down and was about to enter. "May I?"

"Of course. Go on."

Opening the curtain, she knelt in, and Leo watched as her ass stuck in the air, and then she disappeared.

Paul gave a cross sign over his chest, and Leo saw the same arousal on his friend's face that he, himself was trying to hide.

"This is fantastic."

"Time to play," Leo said, patting his friend's back. Playing was exactly what he wanted to do, but he didn't think he and Skylar were on the same page.

"Are you okay?" he asked, climbing in. He had done it big enough so they could all sit together in a circle.

Paul climbed in after him.

"Yes. You did this?" she asked.

"I did."

"Okay, okay, I totally thought it was a lame idea. Clearly, I was wrong," Paul said.

Skylar chuckled. She reached out, taking a couple pieces of popcorn. "You are so sweet. Thank you, the both of you."

"But I didn't exactly help," Paul said.

"You were still there for me last night, and that means everything to me."

Chapter Seven

Paul would have never thought it was possible to actually enjoy being inside an adult bedroom with a fort, and playing games, and yet that was exactly what they were doing.

At the moment they were playing a game that had them putting their hands and feet on different colors. What he was loving was that with the spin of the board, it had put him directly over Skylar. He was so close that if he was just to lower his body half an inch, if that, he'd be pressed right up against her, and damn it, his cock was responding.

Her chest was pushed right up, and he was really struggling not to wrap his arms around her, and pull her close.

"Come on, Leo," she said. "Move already. Paul is looking a little uncomfortable."

"Yeah, I wonder why that is." Leo looked toward him, and gave him a wink. The bastard had purposely put him in this position, and now there was no chance of him getting out quickly. Leo controlled the board.

Leo actually stood at Skylar's head, and now that Paul took a closer look, he saw it would indeed be a very good position. One of them driving into her sweet pussy, and the other filling her plump mouth. He couldn't take it anymore, so he collapsed over Skylar, making her fall, and then they all collapsed in a heap as he gave Leo a shove, landing him on his ass.

Skylar was laughing, and it was so infectious that he couldn't help but join her. It wasn't long before they were all laughing and having fun.

"That was completely crazy, and my arms and legs hurt holding myself up for so long," Skylar said, standing and then giving her body a bit of a stretch. "I enjoyed that."

"It was fun," Leo said. "I think we could have had a few more interesting moves, but there you go."

There was a knock on the door. Paul turned, opening it up to see who it was. Damon was standing outside holding three trays of pizza. "I paid, you owe me money," he said.

"I'll pay you back tomorrow." He took the three trays, and glared at Damon as he saw the bastard had already taken a slice.

Damon held his hands up. "I was starving, and it smelt good."

"Get your own damn pizza."

Closing the door, he turned to watch as Leo passed Skylar a soda.

"How do you feel about pizza?" Paul asked.

"I happen to love pizza. Not anchovies. I hate them." Skylar wrinkled her nose.

Paul rolled his eyes, and handed over two of the pizzas.

"Too bad because Paul happens to love anchovies, and so he always has to buy one pizza for himself, and then make sure there's enough for the rest of us," Leo said, taking a seat on the floor. Sitting in their circle, they opened up the pizzas, and Skylar grabbed the spicy meat one with extra cheese and took a large bite.

"Wow, you know, I was thinking about going on a diet, but when you taste food this good, I mean, why? Why put yourself through all that hell?" She took another bite, and moaned. "I'm sorry. I should probably do the girly thing, right? Have one slice, or tell you I'm a vegetarian, or just go and get a salad."

"Please tell me you're not going to do that?" Leo asked.

Paul said the same.

"I think I've already proven I'm not. There are no better things in life than pizza. Well, maybe homemade. Teri does an amazing pizza. She adds spices and herbs, and cheese to the crust. It is fab." She finished off her slice and licked her fingers clean.

Paul was already onto his third slice as she was picking up her second.

"It's good to see a woman eat and enjoy her food," he said. "I can't stand it when they're forking through the leaves on their plate. What a total waste of food. I don't know who finds that attractive, but to me those men are total douches."

"You like a girl who can eat?" she asked.

"Yeah. I've spent my hard-earned cash on this dinner. The least you can do is enjoy it right."

She tilted her head to the side, and he saw she was thinking about it. "You know I never thought about it that way. When people go on dates, I mean the guy pays sometimes, right? Why wouldn't they want to see the meal they paid for enjoyed? I think you should open some kind of website to teach men some manners."

"You had some bad dates?" Leo asked.

"One or two. I was set up on this blind date a few years ago, and before I even sat down, the guy asked me if I had money because he didn't know if he could afford what I could eat."

Rage completely filled Paul, and he looked toward Leo, seeing the exact same emotion in his friend.

"Let's say it was really awkward to even stay. I sat down, and I looked at him, confused. He simply pointed at my body and told me that I looked more like a 'more than you can eat buffet kind of girl'. Yeah, that was a real low point in my life." She shrugged. "I've had a couple of assholes like that. I'm not a pig or anything. I just … I like to eat, and to eat good food, you know."

Leo wrapped his arm around her shoulders and pulled her back. "You need to ignore those assholes. They do not know what they are missing out on." He pressed a kiss to her head and she was smiling.

"It's all fine now. I'm not hurt or anything." She patted Leo's arm, and turned to smile at him. Leo, being Leo, kissed her lips.

The sight had Paul's already hard cock thickening even more.

"So, no more assholes for you," he said, drawing her attention back to him.

"No asshole." She giggled. "It's kind of funny to think like that, don't you think?"

****

Tonight wasn't supposed to be about pressuring her. Leo shouldn't have kissed her, and he had seen that he'd caught her by surprise. Just hearing what some asshole had done to her had really angered him. He wanted to hurt every single bastard that was in her past, and make sure they never did it again.

She had been so unlucky, and he couldn't stand to think of her hurting at all. Some men really didn't know what their words were doing.

He loved the way she ate. How her eyes closed when she took a bite, and her tongue came out to lick the side of her lip. For him, he was hoping one day she would suck his cock with as much relish.

"Let's play truth or dare," Paul said.

Turning to his friend, Leo frowned. "Truth or dare? Seriously, how old are you?"

Skylar started laughing.

"We're supposed to be having some fun, right? Recreating the whole slumber party feel. Who doesn't play truth or dare at a slumber party?"

"Wait," Skylar said. "Shall we get into our

pajamas? That's what a slumber party is all about."

"Let's get changed," Paul said.

She jumped up, and promised to be back within minutes.

"Do you own pajamas?" Leo asked.

"No, not a chance. I've got some sweatpants. They will have to do, like they did last night."

Paul left the room, and Leo rushed toward his bathroom, removing his clothes, and staring at his naked chest. He pulled up a pair of old sweatpants, and wondered if he should bother with a shirt. If he went without one, would he make her nervous? It was quite warm, and he wanted her to look at him. Damn it, he was overthinking everything right now, and it was driving him crazy.

Leaving the bedroom, he sat down on the floor as Paul and Skylar arrived. Paul wasn't wearing a shirt either, and Skylar was in pajamas, this time a plain pastel pink color that really brought out the depth of color in her hair and the blue in her eyes.

"So truth or dare," she said, taking a seat.

"No, we've played this before. You will go first. Truth or dare, Skykar?"

She pressed a finger to her lip, tilted her head and smiled. "Truth."

"Have you ever been in love?" Paul asked.

"No. I've never been in love. That's easy."

"How about we all have to answer?" Leo asked. "It stops us being a bit boring. Truths all have to be answered, dares are singular."

"I'm okay with that," Skylar said. "Your turn."

"I've never been in love," Leo said.

"Me neither. Lust I have. I've been in a lot of lust," Paul said.

"I don't think I've ever been in lust either. Yeah,

I'm a bit of a bore," Skylar said.

"You never know what the future holds, babe. You could be in lust before you know it." Leo winked at her.

She smiled, her cheeks going bright red. "You never know." She didn't back down nor stop. At least she wasn't running away.

He was happy about that.

"Okay, my turn," Leo said. "Paul, truth or dare?"

"Dare."

"I dare you to go and steal James's phone."

"Are you for real?"

"Totally real. We'll give it back to him."

Paul rolled his eyes. "You're deadly, I'll be right back."

Leo was laughing as Paul left. Skylar was doing the same as well. "He's not going to get hurt, is he?"

"I don't know. We'll see. If he comes back with a black eye, he got hurt, and my bad."

"You are bad and so mean." Skylar gave him a playful shove.

"You'll see it's part of my charm."

She chuckled, and took a sip of her soda. "This is a lot of fun."

"I'm so pleased you're enjoying it."

Skylar started to say something else, but Paul entered the room, tossing him the cell phone.

"Totally easy to get."

Leo looked at the cell phone, and saw Paul's smug grin. "How did you get it?"

"Does it matter?"

"Come on, Paul. Tell us how you got James's phone?" Skylar asked. "Did you steal it? Give him money?"

Paul rolled his eyes. "I promised to do laundry for

the next two weeks, and he told me to grow up. The only parties we should be having are the kinds that involve condoms." Paul pointed at each of them. "I totally just ruined my rep right now."

"Okay, my turn," Skylar said, looking toward Leo. "Truth or Dare."

"Truth."

"Truth?" Skylar bit her lip, and the grin on her face was totally wicked. "Have you ever kissed Paul?"

"What, ew, gross!" Leo looked at his friend, and shook his head. "Not going to happen, mate. I'm awesome and I'm not sharing."

"Dude, I love sharing with you, but believe me, I have no interest in kissing you, not at all." Paul turned toward her. "Have you kissed Leo?"

"Have you kissed Paul?"

She shook her head, covering her face. "Nope to neither, however, you kissed me, Leo, on the lips."

"And it was a very nice kiss, too," he said, reaching out to stroke his thumb across her bottom lip.

"Okay, it's back to me," Paul said.

Leo pulled his hand away. "Wait, let's take a picture, and then you can give this back to James." They all bunched together, posing for the selfie as Leo pressed the button, and then he saved it as James's screen saver. "Here you go. Get it back to him."

"You better be thinking what you'd like, Skylar. I'm up next."

"Can't wait," she said, laughing.

Leo couldn't help it, he reached over toward her, and pulled her toward him, wrapping his arms around her body. "Are you having a good time?"

"Hell, yeah, I can't remember ever being this happy. It's a lot of fun." She tilted her head back. "Thank you so much for doing this for me. I appreciate it."

"It is my pleasure. I love seeing you happy." Locking their fingers together, Leo had hope that one day soon, they would have something more. He had never met a woman that he was so natural with.

****

Skylar waited for the dare that Paul was about to give her. She was nervous, excited, and thrilled to be with these two men. They were so sweet, so kind, so loving. The woman that finally caught them would be so lucky. She was a little envious actually.

Skylar would have loved to have been given the chance to be with them.

What the heck are you thinking?

They are not for you.

You couldn't even manage one man.

They like sex, and you find it boring.

You are no match for them.

Get your head out of the clouds.

"I want you to kiss me," Paul said, surprising her.

"What?"

"I dare you to kiss me, and then I dare you to kiss Leo. Not just lips either. I want a little tongue."

She looked at Paul and then at Leo.

"Wait, you can't do that," Skylar said.

"This is giving you a taste of what it was like growing up, right? Well kids always took things too far. Don't worry, babe. We're all adults here, and if you don't want to, I can dare something else," Paul said.

"It's up to you, Skylar. This is fun, and he's not wrong. Is it so bad kissing us?" Leo asked.

Kiss them.

What's the harm?

They are both sexy handsome men.

You love it when they touch you.

"I'll do it." She went to her knees, and moved

toward Paul first. "So you want it on the lips, and with a little tongue?"

"You got it right." He leaned forward and placed his hands on her knees, looking into her eyes.

Paul was a lovely person. There was something dark and dangerous, yet charming about him. He was the opposite of Leo, Paul being the more serious of the two. Leo was a little more playful than Paul.

Leaning forward, she bit her lip, and stared into his eyes. "Erm, I'm not very good at kissing."

"I find that impossible to believe."

"It's the truth. I was always told that I was awful at it."

His hands moved from her knees and rested on her face. "How about I show you what I want?"

"Yes, I'd like that." Why are you being so damn polite?

"Relax, Skylar. We're here because we want to be."

I want to be here.

His lips grazed hers, and she couldn't help the little whimper that released. That one touch felt so good. Her eyes closed even as she tried to keep them open. Paul's tongue licked across her lips, and she opened, meeting his tongue with hers. She held her hands on his shoulders, gripping the thick muscles beneath her own hands.

They both suddenly went up on their knees, and she wrapped her arms around his neck, deepening the kiss.

Leo cleared his throat, making her jerk back.

"I really don't want to stop you, but what about me?" Leo asked, taking her arm. She turned a little, and Leo cupped her face. His lips landed on hers, and she gasped as he plunged inside, deepening the kiss.

Paul still had his hands on her, holding her close. She loved it.

She loved having Leo's hands on her, and Paul's at the same time.

Both of them were a force to be reckoned with, and they were so close, and they had their hands on her.

Arousal rushed through her, shocking her with the force. Her pussy went slick, and her nipples hardened at the feel of them around her. She wondered what it would be like to have them making love, or better yet, fucking her, claiming her, possessing every single inch of her body like she had read in the library books.

A noise outside broke them apart. She stared at Leo aware of Paul close, breathing against her throat.

"That was some dare," she said, clearing her throat.

"The best one yet," Paul said.

She pulled away, shoving her hair back and out of her face. "So, truth or dare, who is next?"

No one spoke of the kiss, and the party continued to be filled with fun. Skylar struggled with the feelings that had been awakened within her body. She wasn't used to feeling this overwhelmed by a man, let alone two.

The hours rolled on, and it wasn't long before they were all lying in the fort, and she was staring up at the ceiling of their little tent, feeling their presence on either side of her.

Her lips still tingled, and she couldn't help but touch them. Their kiss had been everything she had ever imagined.

They don't want you.

"Who do you think will want a fat cow like you? You disgust me, your own mother. You should be thankful to any guy that pays attention to you."

In the dark, tears flooded her eyes at the memory of some of her mother's spiteful words. They were words that she had grown up with. Her mother had told her so many times how fat, how ugly, and disgusting she was that she finally stopped flinching at the words. She swallowed past the lump in her throat, and closed her eyes.

Was it even possible to believe that Paul and Leo could want her?

Doubts assailed her, and she hated it. She hated how much control her mother had over her right now.

"Truth or dare?" Leo asked.

"Truth," she said.

"Is there anyone you hate and you wish to never see again?"

Tears spilled out of her eyes. "Yes. My mother."

She fisted her hands at her sides and forced the tears back. Tears didn't do anything, and crying was a waste of time and emotion. Letting out a breath, she finally got her emotions in check.

Leo and Paul both took her hands and locked their fingers with hers. It was so special to her, at least in that moment. Then they kissed her on the cheek.

Maybe it would be good to hope and dream.

Chapter Eight

Teri locked up the diner, and then looked toward the large clubhouse. The party was still in full swing even though it was a little after one. She didn't mind. Partying was what she had been loving for so long. The diner had closed a couple of hours ago, and she had stayed behind because she didn't want to go up to the clubhouse, not just yet.

She wondered if her sister was having a good time with Leo and Paul. Those two men would worship Skylar if only her sister would let them. Of course her sister was one stubborn woman, but then it was a Davies trait.

Movement to her right had her jumping and reaching for her pepper spray. She had never had to use it in Greater Falls, but there was always a first time for everything.

Dane came out of the shadows. He didn't look drunk.

"It's just me."

She lowered the can of pepper spray. "It's not good to be lurking, Dane. What the hell are you doing here?" she asked.

"I wanted to come and see you. I'm not exactly anyone's favorite person anymore."

"And you think you'd be that person to me?" she asked, annoyed.

"There was a time that I was."

She froze, and turned toward the man that had been her nightmare, her dream, and everything in between. This was her greatest shame, her greatest pleasure, and her biggest secret.

"James gave you an ultimatum. Why are you still here? Don't you just run away?" she asked.

"I want to. I want to get on that road, drive away, and be done with it."

She shrugged. "Why don't you? It's not like you're helping Ryan out. Do you remember him?"

"Teri."

"No. You don't get to 'Teri' me. You don't get to tell me what you want, that everything is a mistake, and you're so fucking sorry. I'm not going to do this again with you, Dane."

"So I lose you and I lose Lucy."

She closed her eyes and pressed her fingers against them.

She felt sick to her stomach, and she swallowed down the pain of what her drunken actions had caused many years ago, even before she knew he was a married man, and what she had gone through.

"I'm not going to do this with you. I told you that. It shouldn't have happened in the first place, and it's not going to happen now."

Teri started walking, remembering the first day she had met him at a party. It had been one of the first MC parties she had been to where she had met the Dirty Fuckers for the first time. She had been twenty-one years old. It was the first time she had left Skylar alone with their mother, but she had gone.

While there, she had met a man called Dane, and after one too many drinks she had ended up in his bed, and they had fucked like wild animals. Of course in the morning, she had discovered that he was a married man. Ryan had been so young, and she'd had to deal with the guilt of fucking another woman's man.

She had vowed never to let it happen again, and for a short time it hadn't.

The problem was, when it came to Dane, she had a weakness and she hated herself for it. Hated that she had hurt another woman, another family, so she did everything she could to make it up to Lucy.

She had done everything but tell the other woman the truth.

"Teri, I'm not going anywhere. Lucy has moved on."

"You didn't come back for me," Teri said, turning toward him with tears in her eyes. "You made me *that* woman. With you being gone, and now witnessing what you're really like, I want nothing to do with you. You used me to get your own kicks. I'm not going to do it again." With that, she ran up to the clubhouse. Randy was coming out of the house as she charged forward, and she collided with him.

"Hey, baby, are you oaky?"

"Yeah, yeah, I'm fine. I just really need a drink right now." Entering the clubhouse, she went to the bar, wiping the tears away so no one would ask questions. She would be fine. All she needed to do was focus on something else, and not the past few years of pain. One day she would talk to someone, but right now, it was like every single wound that she had put a Band-Aid on was being torn open.

Randy ran his hand down her back, stroking her skin, and she focused on that pleasure, not on the pain inside her heart. She had been a young fool. An idiot believing sex could mean love.

Dane was just a man who wanted to get his kicks anyway that he could, but she refused to fall for anything else.

Drinking down the whiskey, she waited for Daniel to refill her cup. She swallowed that one, and then took Randy's hand. "Let's go and have a good time."

****

A few days later

Skylar got the job at the library and was asked to start immediately. Of course, she was so damn happy, and Leo even offered to drive her to and from work. So did Paul. She noticed both men never liked to be outdone by the other, but then it could just be that they enjoyed doing things equally.

It had been a couple of days since the amazing sleepover, and she couldn't stop thinking about it, or that kiss. She found herself at odd moments touching her lips, and feeling the two of them on her lips once again.

It was impossible.

One amazing kiss couldn't do that, could it?

Either way, the Dirty Fuckers MC were tense at the moment. Dane hadn't left, and he had stuck around the clubhouse.

Skylar had noticed that her sister, within a few days, had become withdrawn from her. Smiling at the right points, but never really being there. Whenever she tried to get her alone, Teri would always find some reason to be elsewhere. Skylar didn't like it. The way her sister was behaving reminded her of when Teri left their family home and didn't return. She had spent hours watching the street, waiting for her sister to turn up. It never happened.

The last thing she wanted was to lose her big sister after they had been apart for some time.

Finally, on a Wednesday, Teri had decided to close the diner early. She was in the kitchen as Skylar came home from a morning shift at the library. No one was around as Leo and Paul had to go off on some kind of errand that they couldn't tell her about. Club business, and she didn't ask what that was.

"Hey, you," she said, entering the kitchen.

"Hi. I thought it would be nice to do some experimenting. You know. I've been working on a few things at the diner, but I don't feel like being there right now."

Teri seemed skittish, not herself.

Moving toward her, Skylar took her sister's hands and forced her to look at her.

"What's going on?"

"Why should something be wrong?"

"Do you remember when you were twenty-one? You made me dinner. Mom was out of the house. You had that fake smile on your face, and you'd made me chicken parm. We sat, and you got me to talk about school, and you'd tell me how amazing it would be for me when I got older." As she spoke, she watched as Teri started to crumble. Her big sister, her rock, finally broke down.

"I'm a horrible person, Skylar. The worst person imaginable."

"I find that really hard to believe." She pushed Teri's hair off her face.

"I am. You'll hate me if you know the truth."

Taking her sister's hand, Skylar made their way out toward the garden, where she had found herself sitting and thinking a lot over the past few days. She took some tissues from her pocket, and handed them to Teri. "How can you think for a second that you're a horrible person?"

"Because I am. I'm the worst kind of woman, Skylar. You're going to hate me when I tell you."

Skylar's heart was aching for her sister. She saw the distress on Teri's face. "Tell me."

"I slept with a married man." Teri broke down sobbing.

She was a little shocked. Her sister hated women who helped men cheat. Teri covered her face with her hands and sobbed.

There had to have been a reason, and she moved closer, rubbing her sister's back, trying to give her as much support as she could.

"I'm a horrible person. You should just kill me now. I hate people like me."

"I really don't know what happened. But I don't think it's as simple as you sleeping with a married man. Did you know he was married?"

"No, I didn't. Not the first time," Teri said, and that started her crying again.

Skylar was surprised. "First time? There was more than once?"

"Yes."

Biting her lip, she continued to rub her sister's back, waiting. She watched the garden around her, waiting for Teri.

"I'm sorry," Teri said.

"I think you should explain your … predicament."

Teri laughed. "Only you would think I'm in a predicament."

"What would you call it?" she asked.

"A complete act of stupidity."

"You better tell me the whole story," Skylar said.

"You can't tell anyone."

"I won't." She sat on the bench, crossing her legs and waiting.

"It's Dane."

"Wait, asshole Dane? You called him an asshole."

"He is one. He's a selfish prick, and everything I feel for him is irrelevant. I'm telling you the truth. I met him when I was twenty-one. That first ever party I was invited to. We had sex then, after we had both gotten very drunk. I didn't know he was married then. He was just this sweet, charming guy, you know? Dangerous because he was a fighter and a biker, and I wanted him. I didn't know he was married."

Teri explained everything. How she made sure she had nothing to do with him when she found out he was married with kids. Dirty Fuckers moved around a lot in the early days, so she would go days, if not weeks or months, before she would see him. On one of the final times she saw him, before they trashed her old workplace, and asked her to move to Greater Falls, there was another big party. She got drunk, and they'd ended up in bed together. "I think I loved him, Skylar."

"Oh, honey."

"I know. Sucks, right? The one man I fall for is taken by another woman. Lucy's a kind woman, and every time I looked at her, I know I failed her. I shouldn't be here, Skylar. I shouldn't be having a good time when she's suffering."

"Have you thought about telling her?" Skylar asked.

Teri paled, and whimpered. "So many times. I wanted to tell her, but what good would that do? I mean, I've always felt that if you tell someone else, it's because you're not big enough to keep that inside. I don't want to hurt her. Nothing has happened for years, Skylar."

She hugged her sister close, feeling Teri sobbing. "Do you love him?"

"I don't know. You've seen what he's like. How can I love a man like that?"

"You can't help who you love."

Teri pulled away, wiping her eyes. "There you go: you know I'm not perfect."

Skylar chuckled. "I knew you weren't perfect a long time ago." She cupped Teri's face. She was worried for her. "Will you be okay?"

"Of course I will. This is why me and men will never mix well. There's just too much heartache to come with it." Teri waved her hand in front of her face. "Ignore me. Honestly, I don't know what came over me."

"You're not going to tell Lucy?"

Teri shook her head. "It was my mistake. I won't cause her anymore pain, you know. She's moving in with Lewis and I'm going to be helping with that. Enough about me. What about you? How are things going with Leo and Paul?"

She knew her sister wanted to change the subject. "It's going amazing. They are so wonderful. We, erm, we kissed."

Her sister squealed. "Kissed?"

"It was a dare." At Teri's strange look, she explained. "We played truth or dare. I was dared to kiss Paul and then to kiss Leo, and ... I enjoyed it." She covered her cheeks at Teri's chuckle.

"Do you *want* them?" Teri asked.

"I've thought about it, but you know that's just never going to happen."

"What makes you think it's not going to happen?"

Skylar pointed at herself. "I'm not their type. I saw Stacey, and I'm nothing like her."

"Thank God. They do not like Stacey, believe me. I think you need to give them the benefit of the doubt." Teri tucked a strand of hair behind her ear. "Have you told them about what happened with Mom?"

"No. They don't need to know."

"You do realize that is the reason you can rarely relax. Even now, you've changed position, and started tapping your foot on the ground. Our mother fucked your childhood. Don't allow her to ruin your chance at happiness. Leo and Paul, they are good guys, unlike some people. Give them a chance." Teri got to her feet. "I've got to go inside and finish the food. A bunch of us are going to help Lucy move. Are you in?"

"Yeah, I'll help."

"Good."

Teri left and started heading inside the kitchen. Out of the corner of her eye, Skylar turned to see Dane approaching. Getting to her feet, Skylar stood in front of him, and shook her head. "You need to back off from my sister."

"I don't know who the hell you are, but move out of my way."

"Teri's my sister, and I mean it, I will hurt you. You think you've got a hold on my sister because you used her to cheat on your wife."

Dane pulled back as if she had slapped him. "She told you."

"You hurt my sister. I protect my sister. You hurt her, and I'm telling you to back the fuck off."

****

Cora looked at James. "Did you know that?"

The window to the Dirty Fucker's office was wide open, and everything that Skylar had said to Dane had been heard within the office. Pixie, Suzy, James, and Cora had heard all of that.

"Well, I never thought that was even possible," Cora said. "Teri being the *other* woman."

"Holy shit," Pixie said. "That happened before we came here."

"It was a long time ago. No wonder Teri's been nervous around him. Holy shit," James said. He adored Teri, and knew that she hated people who cheated on their partners, yet she had done it with Dane while he'd been with Lucy. This didn't sit well with James, not at all. What had happened between Teri and Dane was their own business, but Lucy was also part of the club.

"Do you think Lucy knows?" Suzy asked. "I like Teri, and is it wrong to feel bad for the two of them? Lucy and Teri. I mean, Teri slept with a married man. That's not right. I've been friends with her for a long time, and…"

"What's happening?" Cora asked. "Teri screwed a married man, and we all know now. What do we do? I don't know if I can keep my mouth shut about this."

"Dane told me he was sticking around for Ryan and the kids' sake. What we just heard, it doesn't leave this room, not yet," he said.

"I'm not going to say fuck all. I'm not exactly on team Dane at the moment. Seriously disappointed in Teri right now. If she was drunk or not, I don't care," Pixie said.

"I'm pregnant. I don't need the drama," Suzy said, touching her stomach. "It's getting bigger by the second."

"I've told you that you're adorable. You've got nothing to worry about." Pixie kissed her stomach, and then kissed her lips.

James was happy to see his brother so happy, and so in love. Locking his fingers with Cora, he smiled up at her. He loved her so damn much.

Pixie and Suzy left the office, and he pulled Cora into his lap.

"How are you?" Cora asked.

"You mean because I just heard a potential drama exploding outside? I'm good." He rested his hands on Cora's stomach. They had some good news to give, and right now, he didn't know what to do. "I'm just going to go and talk with Teri." He kissed his wife on her neck.

"Hey, keep your dick in your pants. I mean it, I will bitch slap her if she touches you," Cora said.

"I only belong to one woman." Blowing a kiss to his wife, he left the office.

Neither of them had wanted to get married, but he wanted Cora to be entitled to everything that belonged to him when and if he ever died. He couldn't stand the stress of her being without. He loved her more than anything.

Entering the kitchen, he found Teri standing at the stove, stirring a sauce. She was a sweet girl, or at least he always had thought so. Yes, she was a firecracker, and far from innocent, but her heart was always in the right place.

"I heard," James said, drawing her attention to him. He walked toward her, leaning on the counter beside the stove. She smiled at him.

"What did you hear?"

How had he not seen it before? Teri's nervousness around Lucy. The way she always tried to help the other woman. "You and Dane."

The smile on her face slipped until he finally saw the pain. She was a woman nearing thirty-five, and yet, she looked so young and vulnerable—but at the same time, she'd screwed Dane.

"Do you want me to leave?" she asked.

"Why would I want you to leave?"

"I'm just a club whore compared to Lucy. She's an old lady." Tears flooded Teri's eyes. "I didn't mean for it to happen. God, I sound so stupid, don't I? I'm so fucking stupid, and a hypocrite. I was someone that I hated."

"You don't have to leave. I just wanted to see how you were doing as a friend. Dane's back. Problems are happening for him and for Lucy. I think it was fucking wrong what happened. Dane was married."

"I know, and I know I fucked up. You and this

club have given me so much, and I wish that I could take it back."

"Do you love him?" James hated this. He didn't want to deal with this shit, not now, not ever. Some of the club fucked around, but that shit stayed away from the club. This felt personal. Teri was his friend, and Dane was a club brother. Fuck, even Lucy was a friend, and this was hard, so damn hard.

"No, I did. I don't anymore. I was an idiot for doing what I did. It happened a couple of times. The first time I didn't know he was married. The second time, I was drunk, but that doesn't excuse my behavior. If you need to take a vote and get rid of me, I understand. I'm a big girl, I promise."

James nodded. "This is not really a club matter. Men can sleep with whoever the fuck they want, but there could be some consequences and you won't like it."

"I know. I'm sorry, James."

He left the kitchen, and stared out at the clubhouse that he'd help create. They were all vital and important to being the Dirty Fuckers MC. Dane was causing a few problems, and James didn't like it.

Chapter Nine

"Do I rock, or do I rock?" Leo asked, taking a seat at the diner Friday evening. Skylar was working, going between the tables and serving. They had spent most of the day moving all of Lucy's things into the ranch house that Lewis owned.

"I have no idea what you're talking about." Paul asked, squirting tomato sauce onto his plate, and dipping his fries into it.

Leo rolled his eyes. "What do you think of a weekend away to visit Vegas?"

Paul stopped, and turned toward his friend. "What the fuck are you talking about?"

"I called and booked us a hotel room. I thought we could take Skylar to see our old fighting grounds." Leo was really excited about it. "I spoke to Ned Walker as well. That fucker is still going. I thought he would be dead by now."

"He will outlive us all," James said.

Leo realized that the whole of the table had gone quiet to listen.

"You think taking a woman to see your old fighting grounds is a good thing?" Kitty Cat asked. She was sitting opposite Caleb, and it was her night off.

"Yeah. It's hot."

Kitty Cat rolled her eyes. "You're going to regret that."

"Ned Walker's still alive?" James asked, laughing. "Did you really think he'd be anything but?"

Leo shrugged. "He's doing okay. Settling down a lot. He doesn't do … anything else." Leo looked around the table. It wasn't a secret that many of the deals involving The Skulls came through Ned.

James shook his head. "Give Ned my best. Dirty

Fuckers are not about to take on his business dealings. Not going to happen."

He glared at them. "Think about it. Us, Vegas, dancing, fun. She hasn't had fun. We had fun in Vegas and you've got to trust me. The fort worked, right?" He wanted to kiss Skylar again, and he didn't want it to be because of a damn dare. He had a plan, and when he got Paul alone, he was going to make sure his friend held up his end of the deal.

"Fine, fine. I don't see a problem. When do you want to go? It can't be this week. We're helping Lucy and for once, Dane is on his best behavior."

Dane was sitting at the end of the table and gave him the finger.

In the past couple of days, Leo had noticed that Dane had been quiet. He was moving into the house that Lucy was moving out of.

It had been a rather tense experience, but Leo didn't mind that.

"Sounds like a good idea to me," Damon said, speaking up. "Could be fun. Why don't you and Caleb go, Kitty Cat? Maybe you could resolve your problems with a week away. Either that or I could lock you in a dungeon for a week until you come out BFFs."

"Screw you, Damon," she said.

Damon laughed. "Come on, neither of you have played for a while. I don't know about the others, but I for one am sick and tired of Caleb's bad attitude, and you got one."

"Bite me," Caleb said.

"I would if it would guarantee you would stop being an asshole."

"Damn it, enough," James said. "Why does everything have to turn into an argument with you guys? You're making me feel like a damn parent to you all."

"And we're going to be," Cora said, speaking up.

The table went quiet and turned toward the club Prez and his old lady. Leo was in shock.

"What?" Paul asked.

"Yeah, I was going to tell you in a big kind of event. Flowers, streamers, and stuff. Getting you guys to behave for one day is next to impossible. So ta-da. James and I are going to have a baby. I'm pregnant. Oh, and Daniel, you're going to be voted in as patched in member. We're working on the leather cut, but with the way this club is, you'll probably get it when you're fifty."

James burst out laughing and pulled Cora toward him.

Leo watched.

"We're having a baby and my wife needs a good spanking. Daniel, your leather cut is in the trunk of my car. We were supposed to celebrate it a couple days ago. Life has gotten in the way."

"This is fucking awesome," Daniel said.

Cora slipped out of James's arms, and got the leather jacket, coming back to show him. "Congratulations."

"Put it on!" the table said, banging on the counter. Teri came out of the kitchen to watch as Daniel removed his Prospect jacket, and put on the Dirty Fuckers MC patch. It was a proud moment for them all. They had gotten a new member, and watching it reminded Leo of his own patch, which he'd gotten at exactly the same time as Paul.

"I want to go to Vegas. I think getting away will be good," Paul said.

"We need to turn up the seduction on Skylar. I want more than the kiss."

"Divide and conquer. We both make it clear that

we want her between us." Paul agreed. "Already way ahead of you, brother."

The table got into the celebrations of Daniel's newly patched in member, and of course the fact that Cora was pregnant.

Leo was so happy for his club Prez. James was a good man and had found himself a good woman. She was a little crazy at times, but together they were the perfect couple and he just adored the two of them.

After they finished their meal, most of the Dirty Fuckers went up to the clubhouse to continue the party.

Leo waited outside for Skylar. He had already told Teri that he was waiting for her sister.

Folding his arms, he leaned against the bench and looked up at the night sky. It was a beautiful, clear night, a night full of surprises, and many mysteries.

"You didn't have to wait for me," Skylar said, and he turned toward her.

"And miss a chance to be with you? You're crazy. Paul's back at the clubhouse. Probably wishing he was here with me."

"Why isn't he? I thought you guys stayed together?"

"We do, but we know when a woman needs a special kind of attention, and we know that is exactly what you're needing now, don't we?" He held his hands out for her, and she took them.

Pulling her close, he put her hands on his shoulders as he held onto her hips.

"Did you have a good night tonight?" he asked.

"I did. I can't stop thinking about our night together. I enjoyed being with you and Paul."

"We love being with you, Skylar. There's one thing that I can't stop thinking about though," he said.

"What is it?" she asked.

Did she sound breathless?

"That kiss that we shared." He looked at her lips. "I want another taste of you. Do you think I can get another taste?"

She nodded her head. "Yes, I would like that."

"You want my kiss?"

"Yes. I want your kiss."

Moving one of his hands from her waist, he sank it into her hair, and held her close. Drawing her closer, he pressed their lips together, breathing her in.

The hands on his shoulders held his head, and she kissed him. It was so light at first that it made him ache for more. Skylar moaned, and he stood up, not letting her go. He was taller than she was, bigger. Staring into her eyes, everything faded away as he kept his gaze on her. As he licked his tongue across her lips, she gasped, opening up, and he plundered inside, tasting her.

The moment he touched her tongue, they both moaned, and he held her a little tighter, never wanting to let go.

Holding her against him, he deepened the kiss, wishing they were completely naked so that he could feel her against him with nothing in between.

When the kiss ended, he rested his head against hers. "You have no idea what I want to do to you, Skylar. I want to be so much more than your friend."

"Leo?"

"No, you don't have to ever be afraid. You have me, baby. You'll always have me no matter what. I won't pressure you." He stroked her cheek, staring into her eyes. "We both want you, Skylar, Paul and I. We want you to belong to us. I know you'll find that hard to believe. I understand you already, but it's the truth. One day you'll be ours, and we'll prove to you that we only speak the truth." He kissed her lips again. "Until then, we've all had a long night, and I think it's only fair we go and see where Paul is."

****

Paul was sitting on his bed reading one of those library books that Skylar had brought home with her. It was a romance, and the hero was a jerk. So far the bastard had kidnapped her, chained her up, and then threatened torture. The only touch that the hero had actually *done* was to torment her, though. She found him attractive and it was driving her crazy that she wanted the man who had taken her.

"Total Stockholm." He dropped the book to the bed. Maybe it could work if he was to kidnap Skylar. He'd do the dirty work, and Leo could have Skylar fall in love with them.

There was a knock on the door, and he called for whoever it was to come in. Skylar opened the door and smiled at him.

She was once again in pajamas, this time a pastel blue pair.

"You do like pajamas," he said.

Skylar looked down at herself, and nodded. "They're so soft, and when I go to bed, I like to be comfortable. Do you think that's silly?"

"Not silly at all. You want to come in? I stole one of your books, and I have to ask, is this what you want to happen to you? I can see that it happens." He held up the book, and she smiled.

"Not that one specifically. It's just fun to disappear, you know. To escape into a person's world, and to not worry about anything that is happening. It's why I love to read." She took a seat on the bed. "Leo told me about Vegas on the way home. Do you want to go back?"

"Not really. I couldn't give two shits to see Vegas

again. I did a lot of bad shit while I was there. But I'd like for you to see a part of our world, you know. Leo and I, we made a vow to always have each other's back, and it's never changed, and it's never died."

"Leo kissed me, and he told me that you both want me. Like *want, want* me."

"It seems to me that you and Leo had a big talk," Paul said, leaning a little closer. Her hair was pulled back into a messy bun at the nape of her neck. Droplets of water slid down her neck, beneath her shirt, and it made him want to lick them off her.

"I wanted to know your thoughts. You and Leo spend a great deal of time together, but that doesn't mean that you don't have different thoughts than him."

He reached out, taking her hand. Locking their fingers together, he looked into her eyes. They were blue like the ocean on a clear day. "I want you, Skylar. I want you to trust both of us with your secrets, to come to us when you need us." He licked his lips and decided to go with the complete truth. "I want to spend my days and my nights making love to you and fucking you. Showing you that every other guy that came before wasn't worth your time, or even your effort." He moved so that he was in front of her, stroking the curve of her face. From the look on her face, he had shocked her. "I want to watch you completely naked in Leo's arms and wait for you to open your arms to me. I want to drive into your pussy and fill you up with my cum as Leo fills that pretty mouth of yours. I want to mark you every chance I get, to make sure every single man and woman knows that you belong to us, and we belong to you." He cupped her face, and pressed a kiss to her lips. "That's what I want more than anything."

"You don't *want* a lot, do you?" Leo asked.

Paul looked toward the door and smiled. "I'm not

going to pretend anymore. Skylar, we both want you, and it's not for a quick fuck either. We both want you."

"This is … surreal."

"We can be everything you've ever dreamed of," Leo said, coming into the room and closing the door. "You've just got to allow yourself the pleasure to dream. To trust that neither of us are going to hurt you."

"It's the last thing we want. We know you've been hurt in the past, and believe me, so have we. There's no one else for us. We're not pining for anyone else. We don't want you to change who you are."

"Or go on a diet," Leo said, making her laugh.

"We both want you for you."

Tears glistened in Skylar's eyes. "This is a lot."

"Please, Skylar, give us a chance," Leo said.

Paul stared into her eyes. She smiled at him, and nodded. "I'd like that. I'd like to give you a chance."

He couldn't help it, nor could he go another second without taking the kiss that he had been wanting for a long time. Slamming his lips against hers, he held the back of her head. Skylar didn't push him away. She held onto his shoulders, kissing him back with a passion that equaled his own.

Behind her, Leo sat down on the bed, and Paul pulled away. He was filled with hope, with longing, and everything else in between.

"Do you have a kiss for me?" Leo asked.

She licked her plump lips, and then kissed his friend.

Holding onto her, Paul moved in behind her, putting his hands at her waist, and slowly raising them up until he cupped her tits. He pinched her nipples, and finally licked the path of her neck, wanting more than anything to lift her shirt and suck on those nipples that had been teasing him for a long time.

He moved his hands beneath her shirt, and finally cupped her breasts. She gasped, pulling away from the kiss to arch up.

"You like that, baby?" he asked.

"Yes."

"Leo, pull the shirt over her head. Let's see what these pretty tits look like without anything covering them." Paul didn't release her breasts, even as Leo did exactly as he asked.

Once her shirt was removed, he released her breasts, and Leo groaned. "Oh, Skylar, your tits are the most beautiful pair I have ever seen."

Easing her back against him, Paul held her close, and waited as Leo leaned forward, flicking one of her nipples with his tongue before sucking it into his mouth. Paul cupped beneath them, holding them up.

"I bet his cock is rock hard for you, Skylar. I know mine is, and it wants to feel exactly how sweet and wet you are. Are you wet for me?"

"I think so," she said, breathless.

"Let me see how wet you are for me." He slid his hand inside her pants. Running his finger down her slit, he felt how wet she was. "Perfect, baby. You want this, don't you?"

"Yes. I want it, but—"

Leo instantly pulled away. "But?"

Paul looked down to see her face flushed as she bit her lip. "Erm, it's complicated. I, erm, ugh, I've never been good at this. I don't want to disappoint. You both are very excited, and what if I suck at this? I've been told I don't know how to please a man and I want to please the both of you. What you're doing to me, it already feels wonderful, more wonderful than I could have ever imagined."

This time Leo caught her face and ravished her

mouth.

"It isn't possible for you to be bad, Skylar. Don't worry. Relax, and it will be wonderful." Leo kissed her again. "Will you do that?"

She nodded. "I warned you."

Paul smiled against her neck. "And I'll warn you, you may never want to be with another man again when you've been between us." He licked her neck right over her pulse. "Do you trust us?"

"Yes," she said. "I do."

"Good, because tonight we're going to give you the time of your life." He tugged on the waistband of her pants. "Lift your ass up. First, we need to get rid of these pants. I want you completely naked. Leo, why don't you show her what you're packing?"

Skylar climbed off the bed, and Paul dragged her pants to the floor. The night had only just begun.

****

Teri was finishing with the cleanup when she turned around to find Cora standing in the doorway. Her arms were folded, and she simply stared at her.

"Is everything okay?"

"I don't know. I've been trying to figure out the best way to deal with this."

Teri knew "this" was about her and Dane and fucking up. "Do you want me to leave?"

"You mean run away so you don't have to deal with the shit you've done."

"You've never been one to mince words," Teri said.

"When I heard that you fucked Dane, I was shocked. I mean, we've talked a lot since we've gotten to know each other, and not once did you tell me that you fuck married men."

"Cora—"

She held her hand up, silencing whatever Teri was about to say. "I don't want to hear it. I want to know if you've tried that shit with James."

"No, I haven't, and I didn't plan on this with Dane either. It happened, and it won't ever happen again."

Cora stared at her, and the look made Teri feel worse than she ever had. "James doesn't know what to do about this, and to be honest, I don't even know what to fucking do about this. You really fucking upset me, and it was when I didn't even know you. You've told me time and time again how you hate bitches that steal other women's men, and yet you've done it."

Teri felt sick to her stomach.

"I don't know if we'll be all right about this, Teri."

"Okay." There wasn't anything else she could do or say.

"You ever touch *my* guy, I will fucking kill you," Cora said, and with that, she turned her back and walked out.

Teri closed her eyes, hoping that one day, Cora would forgive her.

Chapter Ten

Skylar couldn't believe this was happening, and she didn't care. All she cared about was the fact that she wanted this. For the first time in her life, she actually wanted these two men. She wanted to fuck, to have sex, to enjoy it as well. Was it possible to do all of that? And with two men? She didn't know, nor did she care.

She cared about Leo and Paul.

They had proven to her time and again that they cared. Both men were so sweet, so tender, so loving. Could they be a little dirty in the bedroom? Would they notice that she wasn't very good?

She had never been able to satisfy anyone in the bedroom. How could she even think for a second that she could do this with Leo and Paul, two men?

Paul tugged her pajama pants down, and any other thought escaped her. She was naked in the room, and instead of covering her body up, which was what she really wanted to do, she stared into his eyes.

The look in them made her entire body hum to life. He trailed his hands up her thighs, going to her hips, and he turned her so that her back was to him. Paul took her hands as she stared at Leo—a naked Leo—and wrapped those arms around his neck. "What do you think, Leo?"

"She's perfect."

Paul ran his hands down her arms, watching as she gasped and goosebumps erupted on her flesh.

"You *are* perfect," he said, whispering the words against her ear.

"Do you want this?" Leo asked.

She couldn't look away from Leo. His body was hard, muscular, and covered in ink. There was no way for her to focus on his ink because standing tall and proud was his dick, and he wasn't small. He was huge, the bulbous head looking red, swollen, and leaking pre-cum out of the tip.

As she looked at him, he wrapped his fingers around the length and started to work it up and down, which only allowed more cum to leak from it.

"Yes, I want this." She pressed her thighs together in the hope of relieving the ache that had begun to build inside her.

"Good, because I don't want you to go back to your room," Paul said.

His fingers stroked up and down her stomach.

"Neither do I," Leo said. "You are so beautiful, babe. Really beautiful." Leo pressed her breasts together, and flicked the nipples with his tongue.

She cried out as that small contact seemed to go straight to her pussy. Her clit felt so swollen and so in need of pleasure. Closing her eyes, she arched against his touch, and moaned, wanting more.

"It's not enough," she said.

"Don't worry, babe. This is just the start." Leo suddenly sank down on the floor. She gasped as he lifted her leg, exposing her pussy. She always liked to keep the fine hairs on her pussy neatly trimmed. Leo ran his fingers up the inside her thigh and then slid it between the lips of her pussy. He swirled around her clit, and then moved down to her entrance where he filled her with a single finger. "You're very tight."

"It has been a long time." A very long time since she was last with someone, and even when she *was* with someone, they didn't have sex all that much.

"Don't worry about it, baby," Paul said, whispering against her ear. "We'll take care of you, and you don't have to worry about a thing."

She closed her eyes and gave herself up to the

pleasure that both men were giving her. Leo pumped his finger inside her, at the same time pressing his thumb against her clit, circling her, and then driving in deep. She gripped Paul's neck as he played with her tits, pressing them together.

"One day I want to fuck these sweet tits, Skylar. I want to fuck here in this valley and then finish with spraying my cum right on top of them before I lick your pussy to completion. I can't wait to see what you look like when you come apart."

She wanted it so much.

Sucking her lip into her mouth, she tried to contain her pleasure, but it was next to impossible with Leo teasing her clit.

"I want a taste," Leo said. "She smells so good."

"Have a taste, brother. Let me know how good she is," Paul said.

Skylar cried out as Leo's lips teased her clit. He sucked her into his mouth, and then flicked the swollen nub before teasing her. He continued to pump inside her, and she could no longer keep her eyes closed. She had to see him, to witness what he was doing.

Looking down at Leo's head between her thighs aroused her even more. His tongue was over her clit, stroking side to side, up and down. Leo stared up at her, and the look in his eye was one she had never seen before. He *wanted* to be there licking her pussy, giving her pleasure.

Again, it was another surreal experience.

Suddenly, Paul took one of her hands, which were behind his head, and he placed it over his cock. Touching him through his sweatpants wasn't enough, so she slid her hand inside and curved her fingers around his shaft.

Even though she couldn't see Paul's dick, just the

feel of him let her know he was as big as Leo, and just as long. The tip was wet with his pre-cum.

"I love the feel of your hands on me, Skylar. Do you like touching my cock?"

She nodded her head. "Yes.

"Good."

"I want to suck your cock," she said, voicing her own desires.

Leo pulled away. "Now that is fucking sexy," he said. "Say it again."

"I want to suck Paul's cock." She rested her head on his shoulder. "I've not done it before."

"Babe, I'm not going to complain." Paul released her, and she sank to her knees.

It was exhilarating as Leo stood up as well. Both men stood before her, and it was straight out of one of the erotic romances she had read. She loved reading about two men or more. Of course everything had been a fantasy, but what if it could be possible?

****

Seeing Skylar on her knees before the two of them was something that Paul had been dreaming about for a very long time. She looked sexy as hell. The smile on her lips gave way to her nervousness.

Wrapping his fingers around his length, he stared into her blue eyes, hoping that he could show her how much her kneeling before them was doing to him.

"Do you want to touch us?" Leo asked.

"Yes."

"Then touch us, baby," Paul said, holding his hand out to her. She placed one hand in his, and the other in Leo's. Both of them held her, and Paul felt within a strange sense of calm. He finally had her where he wanted her, and there was no chance of him letting go.

Putting her hand around his length, he covered

hers with his own, and started to show her how he liked to be touched. "I'm not fragile. I won't break," he said.

"Me, neither."

Skylar had both of their cocks in her hands, and her gaze was running between their bodies, staring at their ink. On their backs, they had matching tattoos of their love of the club. Dirty Fuckers MC. They had put Greater Falls on their back as well. The MC was their life, and this town was where they had found happiness when they didn't think it was possible. They had gotten ink done throughout their life, from their first fight, and Paul had a unicorn on the base of his back.

One too many drinks, and he'd gotten a unicorn inked on his back. Yeah, it was fucking weird.

Still, he saw how much she loved their ink. Her skin was pale, flawless. He could just see their brand on her body, and would relish it as well.

"Do you like what you see?" he asked.

"Yes." She licked her lips, and her gaze went to his cock.

"Put me in your mouth, baby. Taste me because I'm going to taste you." And he would. The moment he got her on the bed with her legs spread open, he was going to taste her. Leo had already had a taste, and now it was his time.

She shuffled closer and put her lips to the tip of his cock. Flicking the tip with her tongue, she looked at him for guidance.

"Use your tongue, slide it all over the tip, and down the sides. Get it nice and wet." She followed his instructions until his cock was glistening with her saliva. "Good girl, now take the tip into your mouth, take more of it inside, and suck it deep." He groaned. "Yeah, that's it." She took him to the back of her throat, and pulled off. He winced as she used some teeth, but he didn't mind some pain. "Fuck, baby, go a bit faster, yeah, that's it." She bobbed her head on his length, and then wrapped her fingers around his cock, heightening his arousal even more.

"Do you want to suck my cock?" Leo asked.

Paul laughed as he saw the intense look that Leo was giving her. "You want her to have a taste?"

"Fuck yeah. Did you see her lips? It looked fucking perfect."

Chuckling, Paul stroked her hair, and saw the smile in her eyes. She pulled off his cock, and licked her lips. "There's plenty to go around," she said, shyly.

"I want to taste her pussy. Can we move this to the bed? I want to lick her cunt."

Her cheeks went a deeper shade of red.

Leo rushed to the bed and sat down. "I'm ready."

She giggled, and Paul offered her a hand, which she took.

Pulling her to her feet, he banded his arm around her waist, tugging her close. He placed a hand on her ass as he took possession of her mouth. She moaned at the same time her body melted against his.

"You're ours now, Skylar."

She hummed. "I like that."

"Good, because we're never going to let you go. Not ever."

Walking her to the bed, he kissed her again, and waited as she moved toward Leo's side. She took Leo into her mouth, following his guidance. Kneeling on the bed, Paul ran his hands up her thighs, spreading those legs, and seeing her pretty pussy. She was already wet, and the lips of her sex were nicely swollen with the bud of her clit peeking out. Spreading her pussy apart, he covered her nub with his mouth, tonguing her, and then sucking it into his mouth. Teasing her clit, he couldn't get enough of her taste. Sliding his tongue down to her entrance, he began to fuck her, feeling how tight she was.

He would need to get her to come before she could take them. Glancing up her body, he watched as Leo thrust into her mouth. One of his hands was wrapped in her hair, as he fed her his cock. Skylar kept moaning, and judging by the feel of her pussy on his tongue, she was enjoying sucking Leo's cock.

Her response was more than he could have ever hoped for. She was perfection, and from the first moment he saw her at the diner on that first day, he just knew she would be the one for the two of them.

Leo had told him how much he wanted this to work, and Paul wanted it to work as well. He wanted the two of them to wipe the pain from her eyes and give her nothing but pleasure and a future to look forward to. A future with the two of them.

Using his fingers, Paul filled her with one, and then the other. She began to thrust against them. At the same time, he teased her clit and stared up her body, trying to watch as Leo fucked her mouth. He wanted his cock inside her so badly, but first she had to come.

With the way her cunt was tightening around him, he knew it was only a matter of seconds before she exploded.

****

Leo gritted his teeth as Skylar's orgasm rushed through her. She didn't stop sucking his dick. In fact, she took him deeper into her mouth, and her body melted against him.

"Pass me a condom," Paul said.

Reaching into the drawer, Leo tossed a foil packet to Paul.

"That was amazing," Skylar said, pulling off his cock long enough to speak. "I've never felt like that or had that before."

"No one else has taken the time to make you come?" Paul asked, tearing into the foil packet, removing the latex, and then rolling it on his cock.

"No."

"They were assholes. Every single guy who has treated you like shit, I demand that you forget about them. They are not worth your time, your effort, or your love. They are nothing," Leo said, cupping her face. "We will show you everything that you've been missing out on."

"Damn straight." Paul moved between her thighs. "Do you want this, Skylar?"

"Yes, yes, I want this. I want it so much."

Leo watched as Paul placed his cock between the slit of her pussy. He couldn't look away as Paul eased his cock between her pussy, moving back and forth.

"Tell me to fuck you," Paul said.

"Fuck me, Paul. Please."

Leo smiled as there was no hesitation. She wanted this as much as they did. He watched as Paul grabbed his cock, and then began to press inside her.

"Suck my cock, baby," Leo said, cupping her face.

"She's tight, Leo. So tight." The look of rapture on Paul's face let him know that when he took her pussy, he was going to be in for a treat.

Skylar wrapped her lips around his length, and he closed his eyes as she arched up, bobbing her head, taking him deep.

Opening his eyes, he saw Paul grab Skylar's hips, and thrust into the hilt. She moaned, the vibrations running up his length, and the pleasure intensified.

"Oh, fuck yeah, this is not going to take long, Skylar. So tight." Paul ran his hands up her body, cupping her tits, and then gripping her hips as he drove into her over and over again. "Leo, she's perfect. You're going to love the feel of her."

He wasn't going to last long enough to be between her thighs.

In fact, he pulled out of her mouth, and began to beat his cock, groaning as strands of his cum landed on her breasts, coating her with his cream.

He shook a little as he eased every single drop out of his cock.

Paul wasn't finished, and he pounded inside her, the strength of his thrusts making the bed hit the wall, slamming against it. Within minutes, Paul was grunting, thrusting inside her one final time.

Leo lay behind her, seeing the flush building inside her.

"I can't believe we just did that."

"Is that a bad thing?" he asked.

She shook her head. "It was amazing."

Paul collapsed down beside her. "I'm so sorry."

"Why are you apologizing?" Skylar asked.

"I didn't mean to go off so quickly." Paul wrapped his arm around her waist. "I promise next time I will take my time with you, and make sure you come at least once. It's my bad."

Leo laughed. "He can usually last the night."

"I really have got bad experiences. That lasted a lot longer than any other time I've been with someone. I thought it was amazing." She touched both of their faces, and the smile that danced across her lips would stay with him forever. Skylar looked happy.

"Have you ever brought yourself to orgasm?" Leo asked, curious.

"I have, but it has never felt like that. Not at all."

"We'll make up for it, babe," Paul said. "First,

though, I think we need to put you in the shower." He looked at Leo's cum dotted on her chest.

"What? I was being a gentleman. I didn't want her to feel forced to swallow."

"You think beating off on her chest is gentlemanly?" Paul asked. "Where the hell have you been living? Under a rock?"

"I didn't exactly think about where I was going to come. Her mouth was so amazing, and I was thinking on my feet. I think it looks really pretty."

"Guys, no offense, but please stop. This is so embarrassing," she said, covering her face.

Leo chuckled and leaned down, pressing a kiss to her lips. "You do not need to be embarrassed about anything. I wasn't thinking."

"It is sweet that you didn't make me, you know, swallow it."

He pressed a kiss to her lips. "See, gentlemanly."

"Let me get rid of this condom, and start running the shower. I doubt you will appreciate a cold one," Paul said, leaving them alone.

"You're not embarrassed, are you?" he asked.

"It's fine. I've never … you know, swallowed." She covered her face again. "I'm sorry. I must seem really immature to you."

"Not at all. I find it rather sweet and endearing." He pressed another kiss to her lips.

Paul came in seconds later. "A nice warm shower awaits us."

Getting to his feet, Leo held out his hand to Skylar, which she took. Moving her in front of them, they entered the shower together.

Between himself and Paul, they took care of her, soaping her body, washing her hair, kissing her, talking to her. For Leo this was a dream come true, better than any other moment in his life.

Later that night as she lay between them, completely naked, Leo kissed her shoulder. "She's the one, you know that, right?"

Paul nodded. "She's the one. I don't want to lose her. She wasn't teasing one of us, while goading the other. She wanted both of us, Leo."

Wrapping his arm around her waist, he kissed her cheek. Skylar, for some strange reason, slept on her back. He'd never known a woman to do it. He slept on his front, as did Paul. Still, it meant she didn't face either one of them. Snuggling against her, he breathed in her scent, feeling calm and relaxed. It was the first time he ever had in his life.

Chapter Eleven

"You don't think it's weird, you know, being with a couple of men?" Skylar asked.

Teri giggled, putting the tape on the final box in Lucy's kitchen. It was the last day of moving, and so far she had avoided bumping into Dane, who had decided to help. She had seen him trying to talk with Ryan. His oldest son wouldn't spend the time though, and Teri couldn't blame him either. Every chance that Dane had to show he was a semi-decent guy, he had screwed it up.

Did she love Dane?

She really didn't think she did. They had been two different people and she had been so young and stupid at the time. Still, she was a little uncomfortable being around Lucy while Dane was there.

"I think you, Leo, and Paul, are going to be so magical together. Do you want the truth?" Teri asked.

"What truth?"

"When I invited you to stay, I was hoping that you would fall for the two of them. You're a sweet woman, a kind woman, and both of those guys deserve someone like you." Teri walked toward her sister, cupped her face. "I'm pleased that you're giving them a chance. I walked past Paul's bedroom last night, and can I say, wow, it sounded to me like you were having a lot of fun."

"Oh please, stop. I don't need to think of my sister being there while I was having sex. Please."

"It was a good sound," Teri said, laughing. "I don't mean the sex either. You were laughing and having fun. I'm happy for you, and of course I'm happy that you're finally here with me." She lifted another box onto the table. "Have you told them yet?"

Skylar shook her head. "I don't know if I can. It's

in the past though. Why should I tell them something that sucks ass?"

"Because it's still part of who you are. You can say that it's not a problem, but we both know that's not the case. It affected you in a lot of ways, and it still does."

Her sister sighed.

"You can't watch a movie. You're always moving around. You barely stop, and I saw the guilt about eating two cookies instead of one. Mom's not here to hurt you, Skylar. She's not here to judge you. I think it's time you gave them a chance, and you know, talked to them about it."

"I better get this box out to them," Skylar said, picking the one up off the table.

"Okey-doke." Teri pushed some hair off her face and put tape over the next box. She watched as Lucy entered the room.

"Can you believe how much stuff I've got?" she said.

"You're sure you're ready to move in with Lewis?" Teri looked at the woman, and felt an overwhelming guilt rush through her. She had no right to be in this woman's home.

Turning away, she looked in the cupboards for something to do.

Suddenly, Lucy was there, and her arms were wrapped around Teri. "I know that I love Lewis and that he makes me happy. I want to live on his ranch, and cook his food, serve him and his workers. I've been dreaming about it for a long time. Ryan's excited as well. This home, it holds a lot of memories, and not all of them good."

Teri closed her eyes, accepting Lucy's hug. You're a monster. You're a bitch. You're a homewrecker.

"Teri?" Lucy asked.

"Yes."

"I know."

She tensed up. "What do you know?"

"I knew about you and Dane."

Teri gasped and turned in Lucy's arms. The other woman was smiling at her and there were tears in her eyes. "Would you like me to leave?"

"I know it wasn't an affair and that it was just sex. Dane, erm, he called your name out during sex, and I don't even think he was aware that he'd said anything. When he got drunk one night, I asked him about you and that was how I found out. He doesn't remember, but Dane during drink can't keep any secrets at all. I hated you for a long time. I hated who you were, what you were to the club, and I wanted you gone. I did. You fucked my husband, and he liked it. He wanted to do it again, and I know in my heart it probably did happen again. When I finally met you, I had this big elaborate speech prepared, and now I can't even remember what it was. The first time you saw me you didn't have a clue who I was, and you were just so nice. You were sweet, and then when you discovered who I was, I knew that you were ashamed, and I thought to myself, that is punishment enough. Then of course Dane left and everything else happened." Lucy took a deep breath, and Teri stared down at the floor.

"You must hate me so much. I know I hated myself."

"I always expected you to say something. I don't know, rub it in my face or something."

Teri jerked up. "I'm not cruel. I never wanted to sleep with a married man. I never told you because I didn't want to hurt you." She stopped, closing her eyes, trying to contain the tears. "This was my burden to bear, not yours. I had no idea that you knew. Would you like me to leave? I don't deserve your friendship."

Lucy shook her head. "No. I don't want you to leave. I know you have suffered, and even though I went through a great deal with Dane, I wouldn't change what happened. I found Lewis. I have three beautiful children, and you are my friend, Teri. You've barely looked at me."

"I don't love Dane. I have no right to look at you."

Lucy shrugged her shoulders. "I only hope he realizes that he has great kids. I punished you, Teri. I made sure that I ate at the diner, that I was there for you to see me. I even made sure I was there with Dane before he fucked off to whatever he was doing. I got what I wanted, and every time I saw you flinch or look guilty or ashamed, I was happy."

Teri said nothing.

"Don't feel guilty anymore. I love Lewis. I'm about to live my life with him. Dane, he promised me once that he would never break my heart. I knew he would, but I didn't listen to my own advice." Lucy cupped her face. "I forgive you."

"Why are you forgiving me?"

"Because I don't want to hate you. I tried that, and I don't. I'm happy with Lewis, happier than I ever was with Dane." Lucy picked up a box. "You're a good woman that got caught up in some drama. My advice though, don't go screwing another woman's man. Some people may ruin that beautiful face of yours."

Teri smiled. "Thank you."

Lucy left the kitchen, and Teri turned toward the kitchen sink.

"She's right," Dane said, coming into the kitchen.

She didn't turn around to look at him. Grabbing ahold of the edge of the sink, she cleared her throat.

"What are you doing in here?"

"I knew you were here and I wanted to see what Lucy would say."

"You heard what she said."

"I did. I had no idea that I had done that, or that I was so drunk I told her the truth. Ryan was so young and I made a mistake."

Teri closed her eyes and swallowed past the lump in her throat. She had been a big mistake. The irony was, it wasn't the first time she had been told she was a big mistake.

Face your fear.

Turning to look at Dane, she couldn't believe that there was a time she was convinced she had loved him. He was not the man she had ever imagined. He was a cold bastard, selfish, who only saw the means to his own ends.

She shook her head. "You're pathetic, you know that." Teri laughed. "With what we did, it made me feel like a fucking homewrecker, and that wasn't me. It never was, and yet I became that when I slept with you a *second* time." She shook her head. "You're right. This was a big mistake, thank you so much for putting me out of my misery." She grabbed a box and glared at him. The chains of the past finally broke away and she felt euphoric. "I'm stronger than you and I no longer have to deal with that shame. I am done. I'm a fucking bitch, a whore, and you know what? I'm going to make sure that I don't have to deal with that kind of shame again." Pushing past him, she headed out into the sunshine and handed the large box over to Lewis, who loaded it on his truck.

Finally, after ten years of guilt, she may be able

to finally live again, to try to find her own happiness.

****

Skylar giggled as Leo turned the hose pipe on her. She wore a pair of shorts, and was running away when Paul caught her around the waist.

The Dirty Fuckers MC was having a party and it was Sunday. There was loud music, and food on the grill. Several of the townsfolk had turned up, including the town principal and her man. Skylar had also gotten a chance to meet Richard, Chloe's lawyer boyfriend. He was a little scary, and he had made her nervous. Chloe didn't seem nervous with him though.

"Hey, let her go," Kitty Cat said, rushing toward them. She grabbed Skylar's arm, and then threw a water bomb at Leo, and it smashed, wetting him.

Letting out a little scream, Kitty Cat ran with Skylar around the side of the building.

"What is going on?" Skylar asked.

Teri came out with several water bombs, handing one to her.

"Summer is coming to an end, and we're all sad about that," Teri said. "What better way to see the end of it with a water fight?"

Next week she would be in Vegas with her two men, and Skylar couldn't wait for them to be alone in a nice big hotel room. Leo and Paul had each told her all the dark, delicious things they wanted to do to her. She couldn't wait either. The way they'd touched her body the night before and last night, she had nothing but sex on the brain. Just thinking of the way Leo had fucked her last night, forcing her to her knees as she took him. Paul had also fucked her mouth, and when she begged him to let her taste him, he had come in her mouth. She had tasted his cum and wanted more.

"They're coming," Kitty Cat said.

Rushing out from their safety zone, they all started throwing water bombs. Lucy was on their side, along with Chloe, Teri, Grace, and a heavily pregnant Suzy. That didn't stop them.

Suzy threw a water bomb at Pixie, who charged toward her. Suzy screamed, but didn't even try to run. In fact, she giggled as his arms went around her, lifting her up.

"I've got you," Pixie said.

"That's only because I want you to get me." Suzy winked at him and envy struck Skylar.

"You little minx," Paul said, wrapping his arms around her, and lifting her up.

That envy went right out of the window as Leo stood in front of her. He put a hand at her waist, stroking her hip. "We got you."

She was laughing, wrapping her arms around each man. "Come on, you deserved it. You got the hose pipe."

Each man touched her back and her stomach. She loved their touch so much. Waking up to both men on either side of her was still a little strange to her.

"No man will ever love you or your fat ass."

Glancing toward her sister, who was talking to Lucy, she couldn't help but think about their mother's words.

Her stomach started to growl, and Leo and Paul led her toward the grill. Within seconds they were loaded up with chicken, burgers, and sausages. She grabbed a couple of buns, and they found a seat that offered them a little privacy.

"Tell me what's wrong?" Paul asked.

"It's nothing. You know, just memories."

"They don't look like memories, babe. You can talk to us. We won't hurt you," Leo said, reaching over to take her hand.

"Trust us," he said.

She looked between the two men and nodded. "It's about my mom. I don't want pity, or for you to feel sorry for me. This is Teri's idea. I blame her completely for even suggesting I do this." She played with the potato salad on her plate, not entirely sure what to say. "My mom didn't like fat people, or any people that had weight on them." Just saying those words hurt like hell. Even now after all the years of torment, she had never spoken those words out loud. Taking a deep breath, she knew she was only going to do this once. "My mom was very thin, and she was under the belief that fat people were going to ruin this country and ruin her life." She smiled. "I remember being in line at the grocery store and she wouldn't even allow a chubby person to serve her. Anyway, much to her mortification, she had a fat girl for a daughter. That was me. Teri, she was very slim, so Mom didn't really mind. Me, I always had trouble with my weight, even as a little girl. She would put me on diets, stop me eating certain meats and vegetables. I wasn't even allowed candy bars. Of course no one knew how much she hated me. She would tell me daily exactly how disgusted she was that her own daughter was a gross person. Anyway, I would sneak food and then she would starve me, and even went so far as to lock the cupboards. She did. She installed locks on the cupboards, bolts on the fridge, and she would make me run around our garden for hours. I would lift weights, and I would be exhausted by the end of it. That's why I can't sit down for long periods of time. I never watched a movie growing up. If she caught me, I would get punished. She would slap me and I would go without food." Tears filled her eyes, recalling the years she spent hurting because her mother couldn't love her.

Leo and Paul put their hands on her back, comforting her.

"Is this bitch still alive?" Leo asked.

"She's alive and well. I've not spoken to her since I left home and I never will. I won't go back there and I won't accept anything from her. When I left at eighteen that was the vow I made to myself, and I will never change it. I would rather be homeless than go back to her." She sucked her lips in. "That is a rounded-up tale of my child, teenage, and early adulthood. That's what I wasn't telling you."

She looked up, and saw them staring at her.

Neither of them had pity on their face. She smiled. "What is it?"

"I want to take you upstairs to my room, and fuck you so hard that you forget every single memory that is locked up in that brain of yours," Paul said.

"Your mother is stupid. Don't ever listen to her. You're fine, and you're beautiful exactly the way you are. You never have to worry about her again," Leo said, pushing some hair off her back. The clothes that had been wet had dried in the heat.

These two men, they didn't have a clue what their words meant to her. Tears filled her eyes, and she wiped them away. "Thank you."

"I feel for you, Skylar. I feel for the pain that you must have felt, and the hurt. You got through it, and you're a strong woman." Paul turned her head toward him, and pressed a kiss to her lips. "No one can take that away from you."

Leo then turned her toward him and kissed her lips. "You belong to us now, and we'll never allow you to feel anything like that again.

No, they were making her feel a lot of other things. Things that she hadn't thought were possible for her. "I just need to use the bathroom." Before they could stop her, she was on her feet, heading toward the bathroom inside the clubhouse. On her way into the bathroom, she bumped into Suzy. "I'm so sorry."

"It's okay. A pregnancy hazard nowadays. It seems that you need to go and pee every ten seconds." Suzy stroked her stomach, and then frowned when she looked at her. "Are you okay?"

Skylar nodded even as she was freaking out.

"You don't look okay."

"Because I'm not. I'm kind of scared," she said, admitting the truth.

Suzy closed the door, and turned toward her. "What's wrong?"

"I think I'm in love with Paul and Leo, and I'm freaking out about it because … I can't be." She ran fingers through her hair. "I've never been in love before, and I don't know what love is." Her heart was pounding. "What if they don't feel the same? Of course they don't feel the same, right? It's me, and I'm just a crazy person who can't sit down because for years I wasn't allowed to, and now I'm telling you, a total stranger who I don't know, and yeah, I think I'm having a panic attack, and struggling to breathe." She pressed a hand to her chest, trying to inhale and exhale.

"Okay, I think we need to calm down," Suzy said, moving toward her. "We need to take this easy and just breathe. In and out, and calm, and in and out, and calm. Relax. You're in a safe place, in a safe zone."

She copied Suzy's methods, breathing in and out and staying calm. After a couple of minutes, she stared at Suzy's smiling face.

"Feel better?"

"Yes, much better."

"I had a freak out when I realized that I loved

Pixie and all the time he was trying to knock me up so I wouldn't leave him because I knew what a total douchebag he is. I don't know Leo and Paul all that well, but I'm not blind. I see the way they look at you, and they adore you." Suzy ran her hands up and down her arms.

"I'm so sorry," Skylar said.

"Don't need to be sorry. Realizing you love someone is really hard to grasp. You've got two men falling for you. It will take some time getting used to. Don't you just love this club though?"

"What do you mean?"

"They're always so together. I mean, they fight a lot, and are always picking on some of their faults and stuff, but at the core, they're a bunch of brothers just trying to make it work." Suzy smiled. "I'm proud to be an old lady to one of the Dirty Fuckers."

Skylar knew if she ever got the chance to be one, she would as well.

Chapter Twelve

Finally, it was a Friday night, the sun was going down, and they had arrived in Vegas fit and well. Leo looked around at the luxury hotel room that overlooked the strip, which he had paid a small fortune to be in.

"This is crazy," Skylar said, standing at the window. He moved up behind her as Paul paid for the service for their bags to be brought up.

"It's beautiful, huh?"

"Beautiful and really busy. I think I can almost feel people losing money left, right, and center," she said.

"It's always a party down there, that is for sure. The high life never seems to stop, not even for a moment. There are a lot of people who think they will miss something if they don't stop," Leo said.

"Is that why you left? You got tired of it all. Sucked down?"

"What Leo is not telling you is that for a long time we were both drawn to this world, a lot more than we thought we would be. Everywhere we went, there was a new adventure or a new challenge. We were fighters to our core and everyone was trying to end that legacy we had started to build."

"That sucks."

"It does. There's someone who wants to be known for taking you down. Then, of course, there are the women who just want to be known for screwing you," Leo said. "For a couple of years, we were both pulled into this world. Fighting, fucking, gambling, drinking, and for a short time we thought we were happy."

"What happened?" Skylar asked.

"James happened," Paul said. "He opened our eyes, made us see what we were doing wrong, how easily we were fucking up. The thing about fighting is, for everyone that leaves, there's always ten more to take his place. We were getting older and the thirst to prove went."

"It became more about survival after that. James offered us something else. He offered us both a future. We'd talked about it a lot but never thought it would happen," Paul said.

"So you owe a great deal to James?" Skylar asked. She gasped as Leo shoved his hand down the front of her jeans to cup her pussy. All this week, he had been fucking, sucking, and making love to her cunt. The two of them were hoping to get her as addicted to them as they were to her.

"I guess you could say that we owe him everything seeing as he brought Teri to Greater Falls and she brought you." Leo moved her away from the window and turned her so that Paul could see. "She's very wet. I think our little angel is having a few dirty thoughts."

"Let's see how dirty," Paul said, going to his knees before her.

Paul opened the zipper of her jeans and began to work them down her thighs. She stepped out of them, Leo still working inside her panties, teasing her pretty clit.

"You're so wet for us, Skylar. Do you want us to fuck you? Take turns?"

"Yes," she said, moaning. "I want you both."

They had done that once. First Leo had made love to her, and then Paul had taken his place. It had been hot watching her come apart over and over again. He had been tempted to screw her in the very library where she now worked. Of course, she had begged him not to, and when he took her to the bathroom, she had sucked his cock nice and long to make up for denying him.

She had loved every second of it, and when he'd gotten her home that night, he had spent a couple of hours loving her pussy, letting her know exactly how much he wanted her. After she had come screaming his name, he'd fucked her long and hard, making every thrust count.

"Lick her, Paul," he said, holding open her pussy, and he looked down, watching as Paul began to suck on her clit.

She moaned. Her hands moved to his sides, holding onto him.

Leo was in a dirty mood, and he wanted this to fucking count. He and Paul had talked about their feelings for Skylar. They didn't want her to hide from them, and he no longer wanted her to be plagued by memories of her mother. He wanted it all to stop.

Releasing her pussy where he had been holding her open for Paul, Leo put his fingers to his mouth, and sucked on them, tasting her even as Paul continued to lick her clit. Next, he grabbed the bottom of her shirt, and tore it from her body. Skylar moaned, and her hand moved toward his cock, stroking him.

In the past week, especially with her letting them know the truth about her growing up, Skylar had come out of her shell. She wasn't afraid to touch them, and she had even come up behind him while he'd been making coffee, to kiss his neck. Having her touch given to him freely was a turn on.

Disposing of her bra, Leo had her completely naked. Paul stood up, and moaned. "You look so damn tempting when you're naked. I don't know if I should fuck your tits, ass, mouth, or your pussy. You're all so tempting." Paul ran his hands over her, gripping her ass and spreading the cheeks.

Leo ran a finger between her ass cheeks, touching

her anus. He'd been doing that a lot lately as he couldn't wait for them both to be inside her, Paul deep in her pussy as he fucked her ass, claiming her completely for themselves. Leo had so many plans, but first, he wanted to see Paul sliding between those glorious tits of hers. Staring at his friend across her shoulder, he smiled and licked her neck. Her pulse was already racing. "What do you think if we let Paul fuck those tits? Would you like that, Skylar?"

"Yes."

"What are you going to be doing?" Paul asked.

"I'm going to be playing with her sweet little pussy."

Paul started to get undressed, and Leo caught her face, turning her head so that he could claim her lips. Slipping his tongue inside her mouth, he relished her gasps. Caressing her body, he slid a hand between her thighs, touching her molten core. He pressed two fingers inside her, loving her cries.

"I think Paul needs you on your knees," he said.

Leo went to his knees beside her, and Paul fisted his cock. The tip was glistening.

"I want to taste you," she said.

Paul smiled, and stepped close. Skylar wrapped her fingers around the length, covering the tip. She bobbed her head on his cock, and Leo added a third finger inside her. Taking his hand from her pussy, he slid his fingers back to her anus, coating that little forbidden hole that was going to belong to him.

She ran her tongue over Paul's length getting him nice and slick.

Stroking his thumb across her anus, Leo moved so that he could use his other hand, and continue to tease her pussy once again.

A deep guttural moan escaped her lips. She

pressed against the finger at her ass, and then forward, obviously wanting both.

When Paul was nice and wet, Leo watched, still stroking her, as she pressed her breasts together. Paul took over, holding her tits together as he began to slide his dick between the squeezed valley.

They all moaned.

Skylar had a hand wrapped around Leo's dick, and he slid a finger into her ass even as she tensed. She worked his cock, rubbing his pre-cum onto his length.

He pressed two fingers inside her pussy, and placed his thumb right over her clit, sliding it from side to side.

She closed her eyes and cried out.

"I've been dreaming of doing this for so fucking long," Paul said. He fucked her tits, and Skylar drew her head forward, flicking her tongue across the tip of his cock.

Leo pushed his entire finger into her ass, feeling as she tightened around him. Her pussy squeezed two of his fingers as her ass squeezed another and it was the same with her hand around his length. He couldn't let her go, nor did he want to.

She was so close, he felt the ripples around his fingers as her pussy clutched onto his fingers. He so wished it was his naked cock. Before they had left, Skylar let them know she was clean, and also on the pill, so there was no risk if they wanted to forgo the rubbers. He was game and he knew Paul was as well. They didn't want anything between them as they made love to their woman, and that was exactly what she was: theirs.

"Oh fuck," Paul said. He slid out from her breasts, and spilled his cum over the mounds at the same time that Leo and Skylar found their release. He came on her thighs, and he rested his head against her shoulder as he made sure to keep her orgasm going.

When it was over, they all collapsed onto the floor in a heap.

"We keep doing this," she said.

"It's so much fun, and we don't have to clean up the mess," Paul said, looking down. "We have housecleaning."

She giggled. "That's just wrong. I don't want to think of anyone else cleaning up our mess."

Leo groaned as Skylar shuffled away. He watched as she grabbed her shirt, and began to rub traces of his cum from the carpet.

"You're cute, you know that, right?" he asked.

Skylar sat back with a humph. "Well, I tried."

Paul went to her. "I made you a mess. I think we need to go and have a shower."

"Yeah, we need a shower. We're too messy," Skylar said. "Don't we have your friend to see?"

"Yes, we do," Leo said. "The thing about Ned Walker, he seems to be an immortal, so that means we do not have to worry about him at all."

"That's not very nice."

"Ned Walker's not very nice. Scratch that, he's nice to women, not to men," Paul said. He patted her thigh. "Don't worry. He'll adore you."

****

"Well, well, well, I never thought I'd see the day that you two fuckers would come back to my gym," Ned Walker said, coming toward them.

Paul felt Skylar's arm tighten around his arm. She looked absolutely stunning in the red dress that he had picked. It molded to every curve, and she had twisted her hair into a bun, with a flower-like bow at the nape of her neck.

Every inch of her screamed class.

Several of the fighters had stopped to look at her.

"We're surprised you're still alive," Leo said. "What are you? A hundred?"

"Please, I'm nearly there and I'm still way better looking than the two of you together. Now, who is this darling cherry?" Ned asked. He held his hand out, which Skylar took. "Hello, darling."

"I'm Skylar Davies."

"Teri's sister?"

"You know my sister?" Skylar asked.

"Sweetheart, you don't get to my age and my positon without knowing everything about everyone, even people who don't seem to mean anything." Ned kissed her hand, and she blushed.

The crazy old bastard still had it even after all this time. Ned had a way of making a woman feel special.

"Back off, old man. This one is ours," Leo said, taking her hand. She didn't fight either of them.

"You found one. Tell me, dear, do you really want to be taken by these two clowns?"

She giggled. "I totally do. I adore them, and I own them just as much as they own me."

Ned nodded. "I like her, boys, you did good. Didn't think you would."

"We wanted to show her around, you know. Let her get used to the place."

Ned glanced toward the back of the office, and then at their leather jackets. "Butch is here. He's still part of The Skulls."

"We're not here to create a war, and last time I checked, Ned, you didn't put yourself between clubs either," Leo said.

"I don't. I'm just making sure."

"What the fuck is Butch doing here?" Paul asked. He looked toward the back, seeing a man with The Skulls leather cut.

"That is none of your business. This was your home once, and only Butch is here. No fighting, or The Skulls will declare war on you," Ned said. "This is a fighting club. You do war with your opponents, remember that." Ned moved away, and then paused, looking back. "It's good to see that you two got out, and made something of yourself. You were wasted here."

"We were damn good fighters," Leo said.

"I know, but this is a city that takes your free will and squashes it. It makes you thirsty for something else, makes deals with the devil, and all that kind of crap. You got out. Don't think for a second of coming back."

"Does that mean you've made your devil deals?" Paul asked. Several people looked toward them, but he ignored it.

Ned burst out laughing. "I thought you learned long ago. I *am* the devil."

Left alone, Paul shrugged. "I knew it."

Skylar squeezed his arm. "So this is where you trained."

"Yep. This is the gym, and you can see all the sweaty guys, and the groupies there pretty much drooling. Nothing's changed," Leo said. "Whose bright idea was it for us to bring our woman to a place that is completely filled with testosterone and, like, seriously buff guys?"

Skylar laughed and Paul just glared at him. "We're buff guys, too."

"But we're not sweaty right now. I mean look at this guy here," Leo said, pointing straight in front of him. The man was holding onto a bar, and lifting himself up. "He's making it look easy."

"You're a little old to be here, man," the guy said, not even showing he was out of breath.

"Who are you calling old?" Leo asked, stepping up to the cheeky fucker.

The guy on the bars dropped down, wiping his face on a towel. "Just saying, you guys have come to the wrong place." His gaze landed on Skylar. "Hey, little lady."

"Yeah, that's not going to happen," Skylar said.

Paul didn't recognize any of the men here. It had been over ten years since he had last fought for Ned, and looking around the gym, everything was the same, just a little different. "I'll be back, baby," he said.

Paul left Skylar with Leo, who had just jumped up to the bar and was showing the little twerp exactly how it was done.

He found Ned sitting in his office chair, rubbing his temples.

"I can't believe you're still here," Paul said, leaning against the doorframe.

"There are always young kids trying to prove something."

"I don't recognize anyone out there."

"You won't." Ned sighed, dropping his hand. "Boys come and go. Some enter in a few fights. They lose, and they quit. Others train, they fight, they get a reputation, they end up dead because they pick a fight with the wrong people. This business is not for the faint of heart, Paul. You know that. I'm pleased you got out. You and Leo, and all of you Dirty Fuckers. All of you were amazing fighters. Loyal to your very core. Right now, I've got a bunch of dicks who are more interested in getting them wet than working as a team." He shrugged. "Did you come back to see that you made a mistake?"

"Nope. I came to have a weekend away with our girl, and to show her where we came from. This was a huge part of our lives. It set us on the path to the club and to Greater Falls." Paul glanced over his shoulder to see Leo showing off. Skylar was laughing and having a good time. "You ever thought about leaving this place?"

Ned shook his head. "Nope. This is my home, and even though all of my family is in Fort Wills, this is where I will stay. Go and have fun, Paul."

Nodding, Paul walked away, heading back toward his woman and his best friend.

"You're right, I take it back. You're not an old man," the buff guy said.

"You got that right." Leo shook his hand.

"Come on, I think it's time we took our woman for some dinner and some dancing," Paul said.

Skylar nodded. "I'm getting a little hungry."

Taking her arms, they walked toward a casino he recalled had an Italian restaurant, and also the means of enjoying some dancing.

"So that was where you guys fought. It was very busy," Skylar said. "It's still got a good reputation."

"I doubt it will ever have anything but," Leo said. "They've got cocky bastards though, and I don't like that."

"We were cocky bastards once," Paul said.

"I've never been to Vegas. I guess I was afraid of, you know, getting drunk and marrying a complete stranger," Skylar said. "It's a dazzling place. I can see why it can draw people in, and never let them go."

"We're going back to Greater Falls tonight," Leo said. "This was a terrible idea."

Skylar laughed. "I'm not falling for it. It didn't matter how many sweaty guys I saw. You both should know that I only want you."

"Hey, how about we do something, like, totally crazy?" Paul said.

"What kind of crazy?" Leo asked.

"Why don't we get married?" Paul looked toward Skylar. "Right here, right now, we make a vow to each other."

Skylar stared at him, and Leo nodded his head. "I would love to spend the rest of my life with you," Leo said.

"Marriage is for a long time."

"We can even fuck straight after. You know."

"Marrying two men. That's not, we can't do that. I think we can even get arrested." Skylar wasn't dismissing the idea.

"Then you can marry Paul. He's the oldest, and when we get home, in front of the club, you can marry me. It solves both of our problems. What do you say?"

Paul reached across the table, and took her hand. "Before you say anything, I want you to know that I love you, Skylar. From the first moment I saw you enter the diner, you have taken over my entire world. I want you in ways that I have never wanted anyone else. I'm not just saying that because I think it's what you want to hear. I'm saying it because it's the truth. I love you, and I will never stop loving you even if you say no."

"Why do you always have to say the right words first?" Leo asked, glaring. This time, Leo took her hand. "What that big blabbermouth is saying is true. We both love you. We both want to spend the rest of our lives loving you and giving you a reason to smile. I hate seeing that darkness in your eyes, and I am determined that before we all die, you will sit your ass in a chair and you will watch an entire movie." She started to laugh. "I mean it, and I'm not going to stop until you know that you are completely beautiful, so what do you say? Will you marry us, Skylar? Give us the chance to show you that we're the only two people for you."

"I know this is probably going to sound strange, but I think I've fallen in love with the both of you. You're both so … different, and charming. Yes, I want to marry you, both of you, and I want to have a life with you, and be unconventional," she said, laughing. "I've never been so happy before in my life, and I know it's because of you."

She held onto both of their hands. For Paul, he knew this was just the start of their future together.

Chapter Thirteen

The following morning

"Does this make me an old lady now?" Skylar asked, lifting her hand up in the air. Paul was on one side of her, her husband. Leo, her second soon to be husband, was on the other side of her. After dinner and dancing they'd stumbled into a church, and within twenty minutes they were married. She stared at the single gold band. It had been on Leo's pinky finger, and it fit her wedding finger.

"Yes, you're two men's old lady. I wonder if that makes you twice the old lady," Paul said.

Skylar chuckled. "It's a beautiful ring." She turned to Leo.

"We'll be getting you a much better one, that we can promise you."

"I don't need a better one. This was perfect. I think Teri's going to be pissed at me though. I got married without her." She had wanted her sister to be there when she got married. That wouldn't happen.

Paul grabbed his cell phone. "She's already on dial, and smile, guys. Teri's going to be answering any second."

Skylar stared at the phone, and then her sister was there.

"Guys, how is Vegas? You had any fun yet? Have you been showing Skylar a good time?" Teri asked. "Hey, sweetie, you're looking happy."

"Guess what?" Skylar asked.

She felt like her smile spread over her whole face, she was that happy.

"What? What is it?" Teri looked at all three of them.

Holding up her hand, she giggled. "I married Paul

last night. It's official. I'm staying in Greater Falls, and I'm a wife now. Who would have thought?"

Teri screamed, and suddenly Kitty Cat and Chloe were there wanting to know the news. Skylar showed them the ring, and they were all wishing them congratulations.

"As much as I'd love to listen to you guys talk all day, I was wondering if you could make arrangements so that we could have another ceremony where we bound her to Leo."

"You do know you can't do that in a church, right?" Teri asked.

"We know that. It's why we want James to say a few words, and to have it as an informal event. Marry all three of us in the eyes of the club."

"It's unique, and I'll let James know. I'm so happy for you guys. Like, big kisses and hugs. Your first baby needs to be named after me, seeing as I was the one that invited Skylar home. I hold myself personally responsible for your happiness."

Skylar shook her head. "You can try and take the blame all you want."

"Are you happy?" Teri asked.

"I've never been happier, and Leo has promised that he's going to try and get me to watch an entire movie without moving once. I think it's a challenge," Skylar said.

"They know?"

"Yes, we know," Paul said. "There's not going to be any secrets between us, not one."

"Have a wonderful weekend, and I can't wait to see all of you so that I can hug and kiss you." Teri blew a kiss and hung up.

Skylar took both of her men's hands, and held on tight. "I don't want to keep any secrets from you, so I'm just going to tell you now. My sister slept with Dane. It's my secret to tell, and I don't want her to know that I've said anything, but I also don't want you to think that I can keep secrets from you."

"Paul, tell her."

She frowned looking from Leo to Paul.

"Fine. I called ahead to the real estate place that you went into asking for places to rent, and I told them to turn you down."

"What?" Skylar asked.

"Look, I liked you, and so did Leo, and it was for your own good, okay? Didn't want to do it, but you were going to leave, and none of us wanted that."

Skylar looked at Paul, and smiled. "You wanted to keep me around?"

"I didn't want to have to think of loads of different lies to come and visit you. Yes, I told them to turn you down. I'm sorry. I wanted you all to myself, and of course with Leo."

"That is … really sweet. *I* think it's sweet. It's not: it's really controlling and crazy, but I think I can love crazy and controlling, provided there's a lot of love and kisses and sex. I love sex." She moved over him, pressing a kiss to his lips.

"You want sex?" Paul asked.

"Yes, I want dirty sex." She moved to straddle Paul's waist. She wasn't wearing any panties, and with how she straddled him, it placed his very hard cock against her pussy. "I want you both together. I know I may not be able to take you both, but I want it. I want for us to be together forever." She reached out, stroking Leo's face. "I love it when you play with my ass, and I know you love it, too." She leaned over and kissed his lips. At the same time she pressed herself down on Paul's cock.

"You want one of us to fuck your ass?" Leo asked.

"Yes, and you know you want it," she said, smiling at him. "You're always playing with my ass. Tell me you don't want it."

"She's already got you figured out. I don't even know why you're questioning her," Paul said, grabbing her ass, and spreading her cheeks. "What do you say? We start our marriage how we've always wanted."

A thrill rushed through her as both men stared right at her. The look on their faces was enough to turn any woman on, but what she loved the most was the fact they stared at *her* with that hunger.

"We're married now. By law you can have me any way that you want me," she said.

"Leo, I think we've unleashed a little vixen here. Is it me, or is she tempting us?"

She smiled as Paul stared into her eyes at the same time his hands moved from her ass up to cup her breasts. She loved it when they touched her. The way they held her and watched her, it was like they couldn't get enough. She had never thought it was possible to have one man, let alone two, find her irresistible and lovable. She loved them so much. Ever since she had admitted her feelings to Suzy, it had been hard to keep them to herself. She had worried whether or not she should tell them or keep it a secret.

Glancing down at the band around her finger, she couldn't believe that she was married. The priest had told them that they were married, and unless they got their marriage annulled, they were now bound together in the eyes of the law.

She hadn't been drunk, or even a bit tipsy. No, she had been completely happy, and full of love for these two men.

They were bikers, they were scary, and they had both admitted that they had a past. A past they didn't want to hide from her. She loved them more than anything in the world, and would gladly give herself to them.

No, Mom, to you I wasn't lovable, but to these two men, I'm everything. They are my everything, and I will never allow you to control me again. I'm happy. I'm going to embrace my life, and I'm not going to let you destroy what I've got.

She felt lighter, free, and full of the possibilities of their future.

Leo moved behind her. He kissed her neck, his tongue dancing over her pulse. Her pussy grew slick as he ran his hands all over her.

"You belong to us now, Skylar," he said. "We're never going to let you go."

To some, his words might sound like a threat, but to her, they sounded more like a promise.

Turning her head, she smiled at him. "I can't wait." Wrapping her arms around the back of his neck, she drew his lips down to hers, kissing him. "I want you. I want you both inside me."

"We always want to give our woman exactly what she wants," Paul said. "Right, Leo?"

"I'm not going to argue."

****

Paul moved toward the center of the bed, taking Skylar with him as Leo went to grab some lubrication from his backpack. They had brought some just in case they were able to enjoy being together as a threesome. Vegas was proving to be the best idea that Leo had ever had.

He was married to the woman that he loved, and within a matter of days, they would all be together in a ceremony with James. This was something he had been looking forward to for as long as he could remember.

"Are you nervous?" he asked.

Skylar still straddled his lap, and she shook her head. "No, not at all. I'm excited."

Paul gripped her ass, spreading her wide. "Leo's going to take you here. He's going to push his cock deep inside you, and you're going to feel me in here as well."

"It's what I want. Don't you want it, too?" she asked.

"So much." Releasing her ass, he moved a hand between her thighs, stroking her soaking wet pussy. She wanted this, and he hoped she would be able to take both of them. "You're very wet, baby."

"For both of you. I want you both."

He filled her pussy with two fingers, and she moaned, arching up. Her tits were on full display, begging for his mouth. He just couldn't resist. Tonguing one nipple, he stroked her clit with his thumb, and even as he heard Leo enter the bedroom, he didn't stop. He kept on licking her body, sucking her, and playing with her.

Paul's cock pressed against her, and he wanted inside her so damn badly. Pre-cum leaked out of the tip, and with his free hand, he smeared it all over his cock.

"I want you, Paul. Please, fuck me," she said.

Releasing her pussy, he sucked his fingers into his mouth, and then guided her over his length. She reached down, and held him against her, and slowly, he lowered her onto his dick. She was tight, and she moaned as he began to fill her.

Finally, he couldn't resist, and he pulled her down, slamming inside her that last couple of inches.

Paul cried out, and she sank her nails into the flesh of his shoulders, holding onto him.

"Now that is a pretty fucking sight. Seeing your pussy filled with his cock," Leo said, moving up behind her.

Paul watched as Leo kissed her neck, and then cupped her tits, offering them up to him like a reward. "You want a taste?" Leo asked.

"Yes, I do." Paul took one nipple into his mouth, sucking hard. Leo continued to kiss her neck.

"How does he feel inside you?" Leo asked.

"So big. So good. I don't want to him to stop."

"He won't, not unless you tell him to. Do you want me in this nice virgin ass?"

"Yes. Yes, I do."

Leo released her, and Paul wrapped his arms around her, drawing her down. Kissing her lips, he slid his hands down her body, cupping her ass, and spreading her wide. Leo groaned, and when his friend touched her ass, Paul felt her jump in his arms.

Breaking from the kiss, he stared into her eyes. "Tell me what he's doing."

"He's just put something cold and wet on my ass. It feels really weird."

"Do you want him to stop?" he asked.

She shook her head. "It won't be the first time that he has put something weird on my ass."

He and Leo chuckled.

"Leo's an ass man."

"I'm getting that. He can't seem to leave mine alone."

"Do you want him to?"

"No. I love it." She pushed some hair off her face, and her eyes closed. She looked in pain and in a bit of pleasure as well. "He's just pushed his finger inside." She sounded breathless as she talked him through exactly what Leo was doing. "He's fucking me with his fingers."

A pause. "Um, he's added a second, and he's stretching me."

With each second that passed, she looked more and more aroused.

"Do you want him to stop?" Paul asked again, making sure she knew that at any time she could tell them both to stop.

"No."

"Are you ready for my cock?" Leo asked.

"Yes. Yes, I want your cock."

"Good, because I'm going to give it to you."

Holding her close, Paul slid a hand between them. It was a tight fit, but he stroked her clit, wanting her completely aroused so this didn't spoil any second of fun for her.

****

Grabbing his cock, Leo slicked it up with plenty of lubrication. With Paul being inside her, it was already going to be incredibly tight. Glancing at his friend, he knew without a doubt that he was making sure that she was aroused.

Once he was inside her, they would be able to bring her to orgasm many times. This first thrust was going to be the hardest, and he didn't want to hurt her. In fact, that was the last thing he wanted to do.

Pressing the tip of his cock to her anus, he started to feed it into her ass. Her tight ring of muscles made it hard for him to push inside her, and once he told her to push out, he was able to slide right inside. He held himself there with only a few inches of his cock within her, waiting.

When she didn't tell him to stop and she was begging for more of him, he gave it to her, thrusting every single inch inside her until he was buried balls deep in her ass.

"That's it, baby. You have both of us. Both of us are inside you."

She whimpered. "It feels amazing."

"Yeah, her pussy is tighter," Paul said. "I didn't think that was possible. Fuck, that feels amazing. She's ours, Leo."

"Yes, all ours, and we're going to treasure every single moment that you belong to us," Leo said.

Leo helped ease her up, and he ran his hand over her body. It was like she was made for them. Every inch was curvy perfection.

"Please," she said. "Fuck me."

Nibbling her shoulder, he looked at Paul.

"First, we want you to come on our cocks," Paul said.

Leo and Paul together played with her clit, their fingers stroking her at the same time. He didn't mind touching Paul as he brought their woman off. Stroke for stroke, he felt her arousal as her ass tightened around his cock. He could only imagine what Paul was feeling, with her tight, wet pussy pulsing as he filled her with his cock. Her release soaked down the sides, covering him with her cream.

Finally, after looking for so long, they had found a woman who loved them both, who looked toward them equally and wasn't intent on breaking up their friendship. She wanted them for who they were, and they were going to hold onto her and make her the happiest woman alive. He was more determined than ever to make sure that happened.

His feelings for Skylar had been almost instant. The moment he saw her, he'd known she was special. He'd wanted her, but at the same time, he didn't want to scare her away. She had been like a kitten, easily frightened.

Now, she was their woman. Their old lady. When they got home, Leo already had his eye on a house, a future for all three of them. He had planned for their future, and didn't want them to stay living at the clubhouse. The clubhouse was fun for the parties, but right now, all he wanted was a chance at the happiness he'd been dreaming about since the first moment he met Paul, and they had both agreed to what they wanted. A life together with one woman.

Skylar screamed as she soaked their cocks with her arousal. It was the sexiest thing he had ever seen, and felt. He didn't want her to stop, but he also knew this could be very overwhelming. He waited for Paul to go first, easing out of her pussy, and when he started to thrust inside her, Leo pulled out. They set up a pace so that they were fucking her equally, one in, and the other out.

Cupping her tits, Leo bit her neck, sucking on her flesh, marking her.

"That feels so good. So good," she said.

"We're all yours, Skylar. Your men, your lovers, forever and for always." They fucked her as one, and she screamed their names, begging for them not to stop. They brought her to a second orgasm, and when neither of them could handle another second, they both thrust inside her, filling her with their cum.

Still inside her, they collapsed to the bed, Leo at her back, stroking her body, and Paul at her front. He felt the aftershocks as her ass twitched around his cock.

"I love you," she said. "So much that it kind of scares me. I didn't think I'd ever be able to love someone or to even be loved."

Leo understood. The pain that her mother had caused her had given Skylar her insecurities. Between him and Paul, he knew they would fight them.

"I seriously thought the apartment rental was going to cause an issue," Paul said out of the blue.

Leo frowned, looking over her shoulder.

"I can't be pissed off," Skylar said. "Well, I guess I could, but why would I want to be? You didn't want me to leave. I actually find that to be utterly romantic."

"You are a strange woman," Paul said.

"Hey, try not to piss her off. I, for one, love being balls deep inside her and I do not want that to stop because you're being an asshole. Speaking of assholes, how does yours feel?" he asked.

She covered her face and groaned. "This is going to be weird, isn't it?"

"Nope. I have a feeling this is going to be totally awesome." Leo kissed her shoulder and watched as her face turned a wonderful red color. His favorite.

Chapter Fourteen

Back in Greater Falls, Kitty Cat stared at the cake she had made. It was stupid, and this was a passion she hadn't done in a long time. Baking was something other people did, not her, but she couldn't resist. She hadn't seen Caleb in a long time, nor had she played at the club.

Since moving in with Chloe, she hadn't spent any time at the clubhouse, other than the parties. It was strange. The apartment had once belonged to Grace and Suzy, and then Chloe had joined the threesome, and now with both of those women moving out, it was just Kitty Cat and Chloe, the two fucked-up club whores who were trying to figure life out.

That was how she saw herself.

A club whore.

Chloe wasn't anymore. She did use to sleep with the men, but since that hot lawyer had arrived, that had all changed. Everything was changing.

Including Caleb. The one man who she could rely on.

No one had stopped her as she made her way up toward his room at the clubhouse. Pixie had told her the other day that he no longer played in the back rooms, the secret backrooms at the clubhouse where some non-members were allowed to play with each other. Doms, submissives, anyone in the kinky lifestyle who liked to play in secret.

The Dirty Fuckers MC didn't deal in guns, drugs, or anything illegal.

No, they dealt in sex, and play, and everything that people didn't want to admit to. There was nothing illegal here though. Everything was legit, and the women who wanted to be played with, used, they could come here to find someone to do just that.

Knocking on Caleb's door, she held her breath and waited. Seconds ticked by, and she felt even more stupid for waiting. Maybe he wasn't actually home.

The door opened, and Caleb stood there. He wasn't wearing a shirt, and he frowned.

"Kit," he said.

It was the one name that he had always called her. She didn't mind her name, Kitty Cat. It was a weird name, and yes, she had been bullied for it growing up and there were memories, dark memories, but she had long gotten over them. The biggest problem was the fact she never allowed herself to be comforted. Being used by men growing up, she hadn't wanted anyone to comfort her. That had been her mistake.

Her past didn't get to control her future.

"Hi," she said. "Erm, I made you a cake."

He looked down at the cake that she had made.

"It's your favorite. I wanted to say I'm sorry. Like, really sorry. I didn't mean to be awful to you, and a bitch, and everything else that I can imagine you've said." She pushed the cake into his arms and then kissed his cheek. She had never done that before. "I hope one day you can forgive me."

She stepped back, and smiled at him.

Then he did something that totally surprised her. He smiled right back. She had never seen him smile. "Would you like to come in?"

Kitty Cat looked into his room and smiled. "No. I'm going to make it up to you and I was wondering how you felt about coming to my place and we could have dinner?"

****

Dane couldn't believe he was helping prepare the clubhouse for Leo, Paul, and Skylar's return. They wanted to have a wedding that brought all three of them together in front of the club. He was happy for them. Even though not many of the Dirty Fuckers were talking to him, he was still happy to see his friends happy.

Yes, he had fucked up. Leaving his family without a word, or even without getting in touch with them, had been an asshole move. Brandishing a knife on Lewis had been even worse. Sleeping with Teri had also been a fucked-up thing to do. Pretty much everything he'd done had been bad or worse.

"Hey," Ryan said, coming toward him.

This was the hardest thing of all. Dane had screwed everything up with his kids, and his wife. Lucy had moved on. She was in love with Lewis, and his kids hated him, especially Ryan.

"Hey," he said. "Don't suppose you'd help me with this streamer?"

Ryan grabbed a stepladder, and walked up it to pin the streamer on the wall. "Thank you."

"What?"

Ryan finished pinning stuff for the upcoming wedding and party before stepping down off the ladder to face him. "James told me he gave you a choice. You're still here, and I wanted to say thank you for staying."

Dane stared at his son, and it was fucking freaky to think how much he looked like him. There was no mistaking Ryan as his. "I fucked up a lot. I've done shit I'm not proud of, but I want to get to know you." He held his hand up when Ryan went to talk. "I don't expect you to forgive me, or even for you to make this easy for me. I don't deserve that. Never have."

Ryan ran fingers through his hair, and looked toward Lewis and Lucy. "What you did was really not cool. I don't want to spend all my time angry with you. I want to get to know you, and if you want to hang out some time, then I'm game."

"I'd like that very much."

"Sure." Ryan walked away, but for once, Dane didn't feel like he was being cursed straight to hell.

Looking toward Teri, Dane wondered if she had moved on. She was talking with Chloe, Grace, and Suzy, and she looked every inch the confident woman he had been drawn to all those years ago.

"You're not having her," Damon said, coming up from behind him.

"What?"

"Teri. She's worth a hell of a lot more than you've ever given her. Don't even think about it."

Before Dane could do anything, he watched as Damon walked toward Teri, and wrapped his arm around her. Dane had lost Lucy, and now it looked like he had lost Teri. Part of him wanted to run, but then he watched Ryan and his two other kids chasing after him.

He had a reason to stay in Greater Falls.

It had nothing to do with the women, and everything to do with being a good father. A better one than he had ever had, and one his kids deserved.

****

"Do you, Skylar Davies, take Leo and Paul to be your husbands in the eyes of the club, and do you promise to be a faithful, loyal Dirty Fuckers old lady?" James asked.

There were a few snickers around the room, but Skylar ignored them.

"I do."

"Leo, Paul, do you take Skylar to be your old lady? Do you promise to love, honor, and ride her hard so that no man could ever tempt her?"

"We do," Leo and Paul said in unison.

"You're just making this up now," Cora said, laughing.

Skylar couldn't even be offended. On the plane journey home, Leo and Paul had both warned her about what was to come.

"With the power of the Prez of the Dirty Fuckers MC, I now pronounce you husbands and wife. As the club we are united, and she will be in our protection, and we will honor your love for each other," James said. "Congratulations, kiss your wife already!"

Applause erupted around the room, and the sounds didn't bother Skylar. She kissed first Leo, and then Paul, and then stood in the middle as they both embraced her. She was so happy, and being with the club, she couldn't think of anything better.

Their love, their support, it meant everything to her.

Teri ran up toward her and pulled her in for a hug. "I just knew this would have a happy ending."

"I love you, Teri," she said, holding onto her sister. "You have got to stop feeling guilty. Leaving was the best thing you ever did."

"I left you with her."

"That's not your fault. Our mother was her way, and she was a monster. Don't let her ruin what chance you have of a future." Skylar kissed her sister's cheek. "I love you, Teri. Thank you."

She hadn't even realized until she was on the plane back that Teri may have been feeling guilty for leaving her behind. Even though they were sisters, it wasn't Teri's fault, and she didn't blame her sister. In fact, she was grateful that Teri had the strength to leave. In her sister's leaving, she was able to find the love that she had always wanted.

"I love you, too, Skylar."

Holding her sister close, Skylar felt a great sense of peace settle over her. This was the way it was supposed to be between them.

"Come on now, I think it's only fair that we get to dance with our wife," Leo said, tugging her away.

Giggling, Skylar went with Leo and Paul onto the dancefloor.

"You're a little controlling," she said.

"You got that right. We have plans this evening. Dance, mingle, eat, and then take you to our special room and fuck you all night long," Leo said.

"Sounds divine."

"Can we skip everything and get to the fucking?" Paul asked, tugging her into his arms.

"You're impatient."

"It has been a couple of hours without seeing you come. Yes, I am impatient," Paul said.

And that was how her wedding night went. Between Paul and Leo, both of them lavishing her with love, and telling her exactly how they were going to spend all night fucking her.

She loved every single second of it.

Epilogue

Seven months later

"I'm the size of a tank," Skylar said.

Paul winced as he looked at his wife. His very heavily pregnant wife. Leo was out getting her flowers. Their little angel was close to giving birth, and she was so miserable lately. She was always covering her body, and she hated for them to see her naked.

He loved looking at her naked. Leo did as well. They were always fighting to get in the bath. He needed to look at getting a much bigger tub installed so they could both share her at the same time.

They were in their home, the one that he and Leo had spent a great deal of time hunting for. It had a small garden, was four bedrooms, a nice large kitchen, and everything that a family home should have. Married life with Skylar was everything he and Leo had dreamed of. There were moments they argued, like when Leo left the toilet seat up, or he left toothpaste in the sink. Skylar was, of course, perfect. She loved a clean home and she was constantly cleaning up after them. The bonus for him and for Leo? They got to see her bending down with that delectable ass in the air. He couldn't think of a more pleasing sight. In fact, he actually left things at the perfect angle just so that he could watch her pick them up. He was cruel that way or just horny.

"You're beautiful," he said, moving up behind her. The blue dress really did bring out the color of her eyes, and she was beautiful. Yes, her stomach was … huge, but so were her tits. God, he loved those tits, how big they were, and when they were swinging in front of his face.

Her eyes filled with tears. "I'm sorry, but that is just the nicest thing you could say to me right now."

She wrapped her arms around him, and held on. He stroked her hair and smiled. She had gotten pregnant, as fate would have it, really quickly. She had been sick, on antibiotics, and of course when she was better, they had enjoyed a nice long lovemaking session. They hadn't taken into account the side effects of the antibiotics, so they hadn't done their job. Whoops.

He and Leo didn't care though. They loved Skylar, and the past few months had been a blessing. They had finally gotten her to sit all the way through a movie. Of course it had been about sparkling vampires, but they had all promised not to tell anyone else in the club that they had enjoyed it.

The sound of a door opening and closing was a blessing, at least to him.

"Leo's home," he said.

"Paul," she said.

"What's the matter, baby?"

"I have to wear flats, and I have to wear them without socks because I can't put them on." Her lip wobbled, and his love for her only went up. Stroking her cheek, he pressed a kiss to her lips.

"Your feet are fine."

"They're fat, and they're swollen. I can't reach them."

"Hey, gorgeous," Leo said, coming into the room. "Oh no, are we having drama again?"

"I can't reach my feet," she said, and burst into tears.

Okay, so it was hard not to laugh, but Paul controlled it. With Leo's help, he eased her onto the bed, and together they knelt at her feet. "See, we can do all of that for you," Leo said.

"But I should be able to do it."

"I can tell you that neither Grace, Cora, nor Suzy

could touch their feet," Paul said.

"They couldn't?" she asked, looking hopeful.

Paul looked at Leo, and they both nodded.

"I'm sorry. I'm being emotional again."

"I think you're being very adorable, and it's just another reason I love you," Leo said, kissing her lips. "Are you ready to go to the clubhouse now?"

"Yes, I am."

They were celebrating the opening of a bakery at the diner. Teri had asked if there was a way of extending the diner, and she wanted to expand. Of course, it was a sound investment, and not only was the bakery open to the public, it also delivered. Their woman's chocolate pie was on the menu and Paul just knew it was going to be a huge success.

"Actually," Paul said. "I think we've got time for a little loving, don't you?"

Leo and Skylar smiled.

"What do you have in mind?" Leo asked.

Kissing up Skylar's body, Paul lifted her dress, and teased up her thigh. "I think we can think of something."

After all, they had the rest of their lives to get to the clubhouse. Being late for a couple of hours, no one would miss them.

The End

www.samcrescent.com

BESTSELLING BBW ROMANCE
SPICY ROMANCE FOR REAL WOMEN

EVERNIGHT PUBLISHING ®

www.evernightpublishing.com

Made in United States
Orlando, FL
15 August 2022

21046669R10098